The Modern Witch

A Practical Handbook on daily magic, useful for novices through adept

Forward (Invocation)

While the mottos of our race have always been, "say less than is necessary," and, "out of sight, out of mind," it is our delight and privilege to bring to you an utterly un-obfuscated handbook on magical living, useful for the practice of magic, useful for novices all the way through adept. It is our great hope that you will derive the full benefit of the information contained within, and that you will begin to immediately practice the instructions within and discover for yourself how pleasant life becomes when you begin to purposefully master the gifts of your heritage.

The Witches of Oak Tree Gardens are three,
The three are alive and present in me,
As I read, I will test, nature's servant;
Witches behest.

***

I'm not surprised by the answer I receive from the online quiz "Which Harry Potter house do you belong to?" *It's Slytherin.* Not because I wanted it, but because I was born that way. Forget the fact that I used to get in trouble as a kid for bringing home snakes in brown paper shopping bags. We'll set that aside as a weird quirk. I'm a Slytherin because our maternal great-grandmother was a *death-eater.*

Ok, that's not real. We don't really live in Harry Potter world, and I'm not really a Slytherin (though I really do love snakes). But our Nana, our mother's grandmother, *really was* a death-eater. They didn't call it that then, and they'd call it something entirely different now, but it's an accurate term.

Our Nana had the gift of communicating with the dearly departed, and of healing sickness. She was known, and revered in her small Massachusetts community, for her spiritual abilities. Most significantly, she had the power to take sickness out of a supplicant and into her own body. By the time she was 18, she already knew how to use her gift, and what it would mean for her old age. When our great-grandfather proposed to her, she told him "no," on the grounds that she'd seen her future, and she didn't think it would be fair to put that kind of burden on a good man (she foresaw her illness, Alzheimer's, and death). They got married anyway, and she practiced her gift when called upon. She became ill in the way she knew she would, and his heart broke the way she knew it would, too. She had the power to eat death—to take sickness from another, and bring it into her own body. There is always a cost, and in this case it was so: a body that's eaten death drives the mind out of the body. A terrible fate; perhaps she might have avoided her fate. But she didn't.

Nana inherited her "gift," and was practiced in its use. I do not know whether she learned from her mother or grandmother, and I never had the opportunity to ask. The world changes quite a bit in three generations; the gift of our great-grandmother, respected in her small-town Massachusetts Catholic community, became, just a few generations later, considered by the same community to be mental illness.

Our grandmother died when our mother was 15, so I do not know if she expressed the gift. I do know that she passed it on to her second daughter, our mother, without warning or instructions for its use. Unfortunately, by this time, our gifted Nana was not in a position to help.

Our mother inherited her gift, but she didn't know what it was, or how to use it. When she spoke to others about what she experienced, she was taken into the care of a psychiatric hospital. Labeled mentally ill, treated with a heavy artillery drug regimen, she spent years trapped in a medicated nightmare. The doctors explained her ability to see and interact with entities not visible by others as "*psychosis.*"

She prefers not to talk about it.

I inherited the family gift, and, like our mother, I didn't know it. More than anything, I was terrified. I saw what our mother went through, and I felt the shame and horror of her experience.

Yet I couldn't ignore it. By first grade, I would walk ourself to the public library, much like the heroine of our favorite childhood novel, to find books able to answer our questions. Drawn to ourthology, ancient history, and the occult from an early age, I read and began our learning through books (slim pickings back then); later, I'd add experiment and practice over the course of years. People came into our life at seemingly just the right moments, giving me assistance or education as it was needed. Years of research, a careful evaluation of the stories from our family, from our friends, and from the available literature, opened a path that has resulted in the book you now hold in your hands. This is not a guide to occult ritual, or a book of magic. Others have already written those books. It is, first and foremost, a **practical survival guide** for the magically gifted in the 21st century. The handbook is many things, but it's also a contemporary translation of an old book I discovered twice; I discovered it in utterly different circumstances a decade apart; this fact being so remarkable I took notice. For the sake of the context, I have kept the title in form with the original, and allowed the original publication date to remain on the cover. The style of the language within is also consistent to the original text (or, as best as was within our ability), though I'm sitting at our laptop in a tech-hub that's exploding like thought during the reign of Lou Von Salome *(Andreas Salome[1])*.

The handbook is a reference manual on how to do stuff. It represents a way of doing things, simply by existing. It contains instructions plainly outlined, and explained theoretically and through stories carefully collected from a wide variety of sources (cited meticulously in footnotes, endnotes, and all the other usual places). The advice contained isn't new, but it is, tragically, rarely applied. It is our hope that this new translation of fundamental practices will rekindle the magic that courses throughout our race. We are witches. We are something different, and we're okay with that.

Ahead of you lay a fascinating adventure. On behalf of *The Witches of Oak Tree Gardens*, I wish you welcome.

---

[1] Lou Andreas Salome is best remembered for her friendships with great men, but during her time, she was respected in her own right. She possessed complete freedom, and she used her magic interestingly and effectively. (cite the bio)

Table of Contents

The Modern Witch Revealed

Who is she? the Modern Witch Revealed

While the modern witch[2] bears no overt resemblance with the stereotypes attributed as her foremothers, we are, at this moment in history, particularly culturally aware of The Witch, in theory, at least. The historical and literary contexts most familiar, including folk, fairy, and pop-culture traditions, paint the portrait of a terrifying creature—the Disney villainess' are an excellent example. These caricatures are heinous and foreign to our novice, fresh awakened to the practice of magical living[3].

Let it be understood that Witches are *Primal Forces*. Being neither inherently good, nor bad (just like non-magical people), witches serve, if they choose to take up and practice the gifts of their heritage, as intermediaries between the "Old Gods[4]" and the new: whichever generation the witch finds herself amidst (daughters of Eve). (*Children of Eve, children of Lilith, cross-reference to Watchers tale and critical analysis*). The witch, throughout history, has been cast in ourriad roles: benevolent, goddess, sacred, saintly; alternately, profane, malevolent, and demonic[5]. While there exist on record many wonderful examples demonstrating the power of good wielded by witches, our *attentions* are captivated by the darker examples, which often serve for teaching fairy tales, and moral lessons of some sort.

---

[2] Please turn to, and reference the Origin and Heritage of witches, for the complete background, history, and a critical analysis of ancient, original supporting texts for the origin story.

[3] **Living magically;** living life awake, aware, and in control of the active flow of the natural energetic flow of magic moving through the witch. The manner in which the witch may write, edit, direct, and be the star in the life of her choosing.

[4] Hereafter referred to as, alternately, the universe, or energy (and energetic flow). The practitioner is privy to the fact that the source of her magical flow of energy is, regardless of whether it's called a Geni, or a God, or as nature or pure energy, within herself—it flows through her, and works effectively at her behest. In the handbook, we will alternately say "the energetic flow of magic," or "the magical heritage," or in contrast with "the daughters of Eve." We suggest that the origin of witches is antediluvian, and recommend that the reader reference the Appendix for complete heritage and examination of ancient texts. The editor recommends that the novice exercise, frequently, the practice of gratitude—wherever it is due, and show kindness indiscriminately.

[5] Cross reference to antediluvian curse on witches.

Perhaps peoples in or from old countries are more familiar with the threat or fear of witches in contemporary society, but it wasn't that long ago, in the span of recorded history, that there were witch trials here, on our very own soil, most notably the incidents in and around Salem Massachusetts. It is a sad remembrance in magical history, the horrifyingly inhumane treatment of what have been predominantly gentle, well-intentioned creatures.

These is, blessedly, no threat, or reason to fear.

Who is she?

The modern witch is a neighborly, elegant, well-rounded woman. She is a gracious hostess, and practices hospitality as a habit for herself, and for her guests. She practices lost arts with ease, and her home is a manifestation of the state of her mind[6]: tidy and well organized. She is an energetic, enthusiastic, and curious lover, and men (magical or otherwise) are easily captivated with little effort by the active novice. She cares for children, animals, and other dependents exceptionally well, whether she chooses to bear her own, and her companion creature[7] (often a notable, distinguished, or otherwise unusual cat) will spend the duration of its life as her familiar. Her tastes are without reproach, her fragrances the finest. She is, to those blessed to encounter her, *unforgettable.* For better or worse.

**

If the lady described above sounds surprisingly *un-witch like,* wait, and read on. Magic is in her blood, and flows through her daily activity with just as much force and effect as it did her ancient ancestors[8]. Let's get to know this fascinating force in greater detail, by first exploring how she plans for and behaves during the day, and then examine the mental and spiritual practices she employs to sustain *Magical Living* continuously.

---

[6] The "mind" is the place we'll refer to as the residence of the spirit (or soul, or eternal energy), and the connecting link between physical and spiritual realities (physical being but a crude impression of true reality; true reality may be seen, but through a glass, darkly).

[7] It is sometimes a human, however, it is not recommended to subject a fellow human (magical or otherwise) to the level of bondage found in the familiar.

[8] The witch is, arguably, the last mortal to carry the blood of angels (or "Watchers") in their lineage, although reportings of surviving Nephilim (the masculine siblings of the witch) have been consistent for many generations throughout the regions of the world (see the text and critical analysis in appendix for complete historical origin).

The witch exists in much higher numbers than might commonly be supposed; this is because, like many other topics of interest, our attention is drawn to wicked witches (they can sometimes be very sexy)--this focus of attention on extreme behavior undermines the enormous amount of good done daily around the world by the vast majority of witches, who have lived peacefully with daughters of Eve since before the great flood. Tragically, many witches aren't aware of their gift (let alone exercise or train it), and if they are aware, use it sparingly, for the irrational fear of draining it off.

Magic is a heritage and gift; but it is also, and more importantly, a *practice.*

This handbook serves dual purpose: to educate and facilitate the newly awakened novice in methods of practice, and to serve as a "coming out" to the non-magical (that we live among). The witch is present among you, and she does better than *refrain from harm.* She is here, generally, in the service of good. Witches have been saints, and they've been sinners. Mostly though, until now, they've kept to themselves.

Let's take a moment, before we move on, to look at the origin and history of the witch, which will greatly help us to understand her and (our) kind a little better.

Origin and Heritage of Witches

Witches are most quickly explained as the daughters of Lilith[9]; and, it's true--the magically inclined *are* offspring of Adam's first wife (also called, *"the daughters of men,"* in contrast to the more common, *"daughters of Eve."*) With a matriarchal lineage, the offspring's parentage is assured. However, by suggesting that there were *"daughters of men,"* suggests the early authors were questioning the paternity of the offspring, and without naming a matriarch, forcing

---

[9] (work into main body) A word on Lilith. Lilith is a title, and may be one of many names, but the title is bestowed on the woman who has a few great loves, a few perfect friendships, many children (of her body or her mind and occupation), and innumerable grandchildren. She is, in effect, the witch who is able to unveil the gift of magicality in her progeny, and her progeny are many, if she's earned Lilith status.

us to conform to patriarchy. Many assumed that the daughters of men were the offspring of Adam, however, the Daughters of Man, in the Biblical and extra-cannonical sources, are the descendants of the daughters of Lilith. It was Lilith's descendants that attracted the attention of the angels (genesis reference, Enoch reference), and caused those otherworldly creatures (angels) called Watchers. So-called because they were instructed to watch over earth. These watchers fell in love with Lilith's girls, and introduced magic and immortality into the bloodline of Lilith. Lilith conveyed many gifts to her offspring, gifts that remain in the heritage of magic. The pairings between the daughters of Lilith and Watchers created a race of heroes, called, in the book of Genesis in the orthodox and Christian traditions, *Nephilim*. The Nephilim were the ancient heroes, from the biblical literatures and the ancient epic poems, but they were also the source of the ourths of gods among men. Now, 'gods among men' is an accurate moniker, the ourthology is wrapped around those whose lives the gods directly touched. The female offspring of the pairings between the daughters of Lilith and the Watchers are the Witches. The Nephilim, or Heroes, were destroyed in the flood, while the witches were permitted to survive. They are the prophets, the oracles, the seers, the philosophers, others. These are witches. Witches provide a direct line of connection between the old gods[10] and whatever domain[11] the witch resides. Ourths arise surrounding witches, and have throughout history, some based in truth, some the work of jilted men (Grimm brother's, and Disney—with rare exception), which is, unfortunately, part of the burden of our curse. Witches were permitted, by the gods, to survive as a race; survival with the burden of a curse: the daughters of Eve are (easily) scared of us.

The witch is, I would like to reiterate, a primal force, being utterly, naturally, morally neutral. She is energetically (magically) neutral, and she is inclined towards good, since goodness is more

---

[10] When one god, or group of gods, retires, new ones rise in their place. However, sometimes the followers of the different gods are unkind to one another; this may be remedied through practicing tolerance and understanding. The same great, delightful truth resides within all of the religions, and is embodied in all of the great prophets or avatars (such as Gandhi, Mohammed, Jesus, Buddha, Gilgamesh, and so on. The editor recommends, for the reader, the book "Hero with a Thousand Faces" by Joseph Campbell.)

[11] Domain is the simplest most effective term, although the term Reality (what we all agree we see with our senses), or Dream (if we applied Toltec thinking), would, among other parallel analogies, including parable.

powerful and pleasant to practice. She is the conduit through which the richest sources of energy (the old gods) are transformed into magical, present living.

The story of the Watchers, an origin and ancestry of witches

"When the sons of men had multiplied, in those days, beautiful and comely daughters were born to them. And the Watchers, the sons of heaven, saw them and desired them. And they said to one another, "Come, let us choose for ourselves wives from the daughters of men, and let us beget children for ourselves" (1 Enoch 6:1-2).

The Witches, an Origin Tale

The gods created the earth, and all the things in the earth, and gave animals of like kind one to another, commanding them to multiply and fill up the earth. The gods also gave mankind, male and female, to each other commanding them also, *multiply.* Among the race of men, there were two lineages: the daughters of Eve, called the daughters of god, and the daughters of Lilith, called daughters of men. But for angels, where was their like? Angels were made male, and females were none. The angels entertained themselves by watching the earth, and came to be called *Watchers.*

After some time, as earth filled up with men and animals, the angels looked around the earth, and said one to another, *"All life has been given the command, "multiply and fill up the earth," but to us, the gods have given no females."* So the angels again looked around the earth, and they saw that the daughters of men were beautiful; once the angels looked upon them, they could not look away, but burned with desire to possess them. And it came to pass that the angels took to wife the daughters of men, and fathered a race of peoples.

The angels taught their wives things unknown to the daughters of god: oursterious arts, bewitching music, and the secrets of cosmetics. Children born of these pairings are, first, the heroes of renown, giants among men, handsome and brave warriors called *Nephilim*. Feared by men and loved by the daughters of men and god, these sons became so great that they surpassed men in all things—including wickedness.

Also born of the union between the daughters of men and angels are the *Witches*. These women possessed the beauty, skills, and talents of their mothers, and are, unlike their brothers the Nephilim, gifted with *magic*.

After a time, the angels saw their wives, their sons, and their daughters, and said to one another, *"If the gods look upon the earth, and see what we have done, surely they will punish us, since our wives, daughters and sons have all the good things of the earth for themselves, leaving the sons of god little better off than animals."* They were afraid.

The angels called Enoch, beloved of the gods, saying, *"Go to the gods on our behalf, and tell them what we have done. Intercede for us, so that they will not be angry with us and punish us, or destroy us or our families for what we have done."*

Enoch went before the gods. *"The angels have taken as wives the daughters of men, teaching them secrets hitherto unknown. Their sons are giants in the land, consuming that which they have not sown, and their daughters are magic, mesmerizing the sons and daughters of god."*

The gods were angered, and said, *"Destroy it all, and begin again, for our creation has been ruined by this thing that the Watchers have done."*

14

But Enoch answered the gods, interceding on the angels' behalf, saying, and *"Surely there is another way?"*

Because of the love born Enoch by the gods, they considered his plea, then rendered judgment, saying, *"Let the daughters of men become barren, so that the sons will not be born to them again. The Nephilim, because of their wickedness, shall die in a great flood, and their spirits will roam the earth until the end of time. Let them pester wicked men so they will know how the gods view wickedness. Let the Witches live, but let them be feared by the sons and daughters of god. And let the angels watch, that they may see all the trouble they have caused."*

Note* the good news is that the witches survive every, and any, apocalypse—novice, if you find yourself amidst an apocalypse, take heart.

(Please visit the appendix to read the origin story, as extracted from the Pseudoepigrapha texts from Enoch 1-26)

Putting the handbook to the test

The practices are effective, for "reason must be our last judge and guide in everything (John Locke, <u>An Essay Concerning Human Understanding</u>)." And, once reason has been satisfied, I recommend mixing it with good dose of faith—instructions as to how to accomplish this are included. The contents of the handbook are first and foremost practical; the methods and practices suggested within have been thoroughly tested, and for the curious reader, we have below described the method of testing employed throughout the process of delivering the handbook to readers.

We may acquire knowledge, according to the classical theories, in one of two methods: rationalism (reason is enough to know if a thing is true or not), and empiricism (gaining knowledge through the perception of our five—or six—senses). An empirically tested truth is one that has manifested evidence of its truth into physical reality. While the mind alone may discover truth through rationalism $(1+1=2)$, truths, when actively applied to daily living, must meet *both* requirements. What begins in thought, enters the sense perception, then may again enter that higher realm of universal truth. Let us engage reason, and create a "bridge between the two worlds of being and becoming (Pojman 36)."

The editor put to practical test, the advice found within the handbook throughout the writing process, since some of the advice seemed a little… well, too good to be true, and felt that it would be valuable to include practical examples of how the witch succeeds in magical living. So, for the sake of providing solid examples, I will interject throughout the text with descriptions of the tests (whether tests of reason, or tests of the five acknowledged senses) and the results performed by your willing editor during that time. These practical resources take the form of interjections within the main body of text, are labeled as follows:

1. Tested with Reason, 001 (002, 003, et cetera)

2. Tested Empirically, 001 (002, 003, et cetera)

3. Practical Application, 001 (002, 003, et cetera)

Each of these is explained in greater detail, below.

- **Tested with Reason, 001 (002, 003, et cetera).** These are the sections where an interjection of a reasonable, logical argument that can be demonstrated by shifting the perspective (parable, analogy, or metaphor), and uses standard arguments of reason is made.

- **Tested Empirically, (002, 003, et cetera).** Actual physical manifestations perceptible to one of the five acknowledged senses, as a result of practical testing conducted by ourself (and/or by our intimates) during the writing process of *The Modern Witch.*

- **Practical application, 001 (002, etc)**

  Lessons from the Magical, which are life lessons, either lessons which demonstrate with reason or empirically demonstrated, from great, magical leaders throughout history. While there is only a small selection represented in the Modern Witch, the lessons are the ones most generally and universally applicable.

  > "I have simply tried in our own way to apply the eternal truths to our daily life and problems"
  > "After long study and experience, I have come to the conclusion that [1] all religions are true; [2] all religions have some error in them; [3] all religions are almost as dear to me as our own Hinduism, in as much as all human beings should be as dear to one as one's own close relatives. Our own veneration for other faiths is the same as that for our own faith; therefore no thought of conversion is possible."[

After reviewing the recorded results of the tests, and reviewing the examples demonstrated and recorded in history, the reader may judge for themselves, or begin to apply practical experiments on their own accord (most highly recommended). Practice is, in this case, merely *putting to practical test* the advice found within.

Now to the burning question that certainly is at the forefront of your mind: *are you a witch?*

Part One: Are you a Witch?

If you've picked up this book, then you might be a witch.

Awaking to the flow of magic

Welcome to the *"Choose Your Own Adventure"* tale that is living with magic. Awaking to magic, whatever the cause of your awakening, can be compared to waking up and realizing that you are the heroine of a *Choose Your Own Adventure* story. *The Modern Witch* has been prepared to serve as a practical, testable, usable handbook, to assist the novice in the practice of magical living.

"Thou hast made known to me the ways of life; thou wilt make me full of gladness with thy presence."

It feels good to be filled with magic.

The witch will awaken to the energetic flow of magic inherent within, she may begin practicing magical living immediately. It is a way of life, and it does, indeed, fill the witch with gladness, this positive and pleasant flow of energy, and it need not be relegated to ourstical or religious experience.

Releasing the flow of magic

Just as the archaeologist breaks an ancient vessel to reveal pricelss scrolls within, so the novice may discover her "awakening" comes during of immediately following a particularly difficult circumstance (*breaking)* of her own.

"The turning point in the lives of those who succeed usually comes at the moment of some crisis, through which they are introduced to their "other selves" (Hill 34)."

This *other self* is the result of the process of having been broken (emotionally or physically), and the release of flow of magic often follows thereafter. The magical lineage will make itself apparent during crisis, or in response to dramatic life changes.

Any adversity, setback, or perceived failure, can be viewed as a pinch, inviting us to awaken. And when the novice *does* so, it is to the flow of magic, at which point she may begin to practice magical living. It is both sorrowful and joyful, this process. Use the *break* as an advantage. It's an opportunity. Wherever you may find yourself when this happens, simply begin where you are, and then begin to focus on where you are going. For those riders out there (so many of us are), it's just gathering up the reins.

For the non-riders, take the advice of the ancient poet-king Solomon,

"Let your eyes look ahead, and let your gaze be fixed straight in front of you.[12] "

The call of magic

Your heritage as a witch, and your gift, should you choose to practice, is to keep the greatest story ever told moving along. It becomes your story when you pick up and play your role actively. By embracing your heritage and accepting the role of player (opposed to pawn) in the great history of our species. Witches have a long heritage, and have been players throughout recorded history and pre-history. It is your opportunity to take up where our ancestresses left off, to return the magically gifted to the visible living, and prove, once

Desire to practice is more important than magical heritage, though magicality helps.

and for all, that not only are we *not* wicked, or green, or warty, we are, in fact, here to help the human race as a whole progress forward. The ancient magic of the witch co-mingled with the powerful knowledge of science creates a unique opportunity in which, together, we might advance humanity leaps and bounds. With the empirical measuring tools now available to us, we can put magic to use with reliable, reproducible results! This is excellent news, and now that we are *out,* we have the opportunity to work quickly for the benefit of all. But first, *you must choose.*

---

[12] NASB, Proverbs 4:25

People who "look back" may find themselves frozen in place—unable to move forward in the living of life (such as Lot's Wife, who turned into a pillar of salt for looking back on her lost home in Sodom and Gommorah, reference).

Many call on magic, and many receive the awakening call of the flow of magic. *However*, few take the next, vital step, which is *choosing*.

There is a translation, or perhaps understanding, error present in well-known Bible verse,

"Many are called, few are chosen."

What some *hear* is that a select few are predestined to be picked by "God", and are, therefore, *Chosen*. The truth requires more personal responsibility, but it is a wonderful truth, and it is this: the one who calls on magic, *chooses*. They choose, and because of this *their status* becomes *"Chosen."* As in, *"this one has chosen."* Permit me to emphasize and reiterate: not making an active choice *is the same as choosing "no.*[13]*"*

Conquer fear, and simply choose; honestly, *what* the novice may choose is completely up to her, and it should be a delightful and happy choice, and it will be, so long as it is the novice who is doing the choosing for herself. Not many trust their dinner-date to order for them off of the menu in a restaurant, why would you trust someone else with the story of your life? Your life, novice, is the performance of a lifetime. It is your performance, and it is a walk-on role that you are inherently perfect for. When you begin to become self-referential—when you look to yourself for your own opinion, to know your own desires, you are practicing control over your performance.

You get to decide whether it immortalizes you, whether it's worthy of you. You choose the results, and what you do with everything in-between.

the in-between (topical expansion). it's what occurs during the *in-between* moments that really count; where magic happens, and magical living exists and is sustained. Enjoy this moment, for this moment is your life (citation-fridge pic)

[131313] Not making an active choice is the same as choosing "no," and not choosing is effectively giving up your power to determine your destiny, your reality. We wish good luck to these souls.

Who can Practice? Using magic effectively

The wonderful news for the reader is that, regardless of whether you are in possession of the magical lineage, you may, if you choose, *practice magical living* anyway. *The Modern Witch* is handbook, and the principles outlined within the handbook may be applied and practiced with or without the natural gift for magic. While many elements of practice are *easier* for the natural witch, all of the practices within the witch's tool-box are available, and useful, to any and all who wish to employ said practice.

Mitochondrial DNA carries the gene for magicality.

"X" marks the spot!

Use of feminine pronouns

Additionally, throughout the text, the reader will notice that the pronoun *"she"* has been used exclusively. The reason for this is, simply, that magicality is transmitted through the matriarchal line: through the X chromosome[14]. Every human on earth possess *at least one* X chromosome, and the person who happens to possess, in addition to their X chromosome, a Y, should take heart, and be encouraged in the practical application of the advice outlined here for useful edification and instruction in magical living. Magically is transmitted through the matriarchal line, simply because is the only way to ensure that it survives in homo sapient. "X" marks the spot, and this is where magical energy directs its flow and attention. Male practitioners understand this quite well; coming into the practice of magical living required them to, at some juncture, acknowledge and accept their feminine side (it's in all of us, pesky chromosome!)[15]. The complete heritage of the magicality of witches has been conveniently supplied in the appendix[16], along with a scholarly analysis[17] of the ancient texts that provide the historical data referenced in the origin account.

---

[14] Mitochondrial DNA

[15] Any chromosomal anomalies within the mortal coil generate an astounding magnet for magical energy. Such persons are blessed if and when they learn to practice.

[16] The Watchers, story of

[17] A critical analysis of Genesis 6:1 and the book 1 Enoch 1-26

This handbook will introduce the novice practitioner, whether magically gifted (a witch), or otherwise, to the art and practice of magic. While our objective and driving purpose is to identify and encourage the novice witch, we hope that every reader will benefit from the wonderful practice of magical living.

Signs you may be coming into your powers

You may begin to recognize that you are coming into your powers if:

1. You have been surprised to discover that you no longer fear spiders?

2. You no longer suffer irrational fears in general?

3. Snakes seem cute and interesting?

4. Some crisis has opened up a flood of powerful feeling?

5. You have suddenly begun to understand some information or situation with clarity?

6. You have been having unusual dreams or premonitions?

7. Things you think about begun to come true?

8. Your interests, always far-ranging, suddenly find focus

9. inexplicable events surround you

These are a few of the many signs that you are, in fact, in possession of the magical lineage (See "Origin and Heritage of Witches," p._}. You are coming into your powers as a witch, and you must take the time to educate yourself so that you may practice mastery over, and actively choose what to do with these new powers.

Tested Empirically, 001

A few well-intentioned words for the newly awakened novice: wakeup and breakup/ breakup and wakeup, or any traumatic event, may jolt your powers to the surface—you instinctively reach for them during difficult times, and the more difficult the challenge you are facing, the greater the power that answers your call. Whatever it was that caused this, remember that time heals all wounds, and we learn valuable lessons from our scars. So, embrace healing and use it as an opportunity to begin magical living. When the novice first "wakes" to the magic, she may experience a drunken sensation, similar to that which we see when the newborn foal stands for the first time on its spindly legs. The good news is, this sensation passes quickly, as the novice acclimates to the new elevation which she was, incidentally, born to.

"You have been disappointed, you have undergone defeat... you have felt he great heart within you crushed until it bled. Take courage, for these experiences have tempered the spiritual metal of which you are made—they are assets of incomparable value (Hill 33)."

Living life as a witch

Sometimes, life is hard. Take these opportunities to get some cleaning done. Taking charge of even the smallest area of life can help you to remember that you are in control of all of your life. Disappointments will pile up when you attempt to control others, so I recommend that you focus on what you are able to effect—namely, your attitude and your actions. When you do this, you will discover that you have easily secured the cooperation of exactly the right person/people to your cause. "You already know everyone that you need to." (cite) Magic works during the most mundane moments, and it is in these in-between moments where we learn the true power of magical living.

I suggest, heartily, that the novice begin to put the information provided here into effect immediately as a "practical test." Begin anywhere, and practice, then keep practicing. The good news is that the practices outlined in the handbook *survive empirical testing.*

Living magically is achieved through the application of a useful set of practices, through which we secure dominion over every area of our lives. Successful practice belongs to those who are prepared to receive, and take responsibility, for the flow of magic which is abundant, and *already present and working within the witch.* That is, beginning to direct the course of the energetic flow of magic at will, *and always at will.*

Part of living magically means understanding that every thought, every word, every action, is charged with *energy* and will result in definite consequences; once you understand this, you may begin to live differently, to behave differently. Exercising mastery over your emotions, through mindful practice, is one of the keys to living with courage, unscathed by setbacks or failures. This is the keystone upon which magical life is built. Certain outward signs (of magic present) will manifest, slowly at first, then at an accelerating pace, whether in physical objects (visibly display of new found success or wealth) or in the style of life practiced by the witch. Provided within is information relating to the common, daily life of the modern witch (see "lifestyle revealed"), which we hope will demonstrate an ideal worthy of the novice to emulate.

Have you ever thought that someone you love is wasting their potential? Embrace courage, and begin magical living, it will infect them too.

Whatever it is that the novice chooses to occupy her energies doing, let her learn to trust her own conscience; this guide will always lead her along well-lit paths, even if the path may seem dark to another view. Just follow the light of your own inner lamp, novice, and you will soon see that the path you choose is taking you where it is you want to go.

An interjection on the dangers of looking back:

When the novice decides to follow her own path, that path may not be the path her family and friends, or others, thought that she would take. They may express genuine concern, or they may even actively try to intervene to "protect" her from failure. The person who expects to fail will, but the practicing novice has begun to see that tripping on the path is simply a result of not paying attention to her feet. At times, the path may be lonely, as she transitions between what she was going before into where she is going, but rest assured! There is always help along the way at just the right time (magic cares for its own), and sometimes the will-power will be tested. Just remember, each of life's tests are meant to simply assess progress, and we all fail some of the tests. Failure itself is a test, and once the novice passes that test—she is empowered to move on with the wisdom from the lesson. Failure is a lesson best learned quickly, and left behind!

The novice who gets on her path, and spends her energy looking back from the road she left behind, may discover herself tripping and falling all over the place. Look forward to move forward, look backward and be held back. It's quite simple, and with a little discipline, the novice may train herself to always be looking forward.

Living magically is a wondrous thing; however, the novice might, for whatever reason, feel afraid, or worry that she is *not worthy* of a "magical life." A quick way to get started with magical living, even if you feel you aren't ready for it, is to embrace it for someone you have strong feelings about—someone you love. Magical living affects the people around us (it rubs off); have the confidence of belief *for yourself,* you may develop confidence and decide to live magically to show someone else that it is possible, and to inspire that person or persons. *Show and tell:* here is a helpful tip—the only way to effectively share magical living with anyone at all, whether it is with your friends or your family, or with hundreds, or thousands, or even millions, is to *show.* Showing magical living sends out a "call" to the magicality present in the blood and heritage of natural witches, and ignites the curiosity of the daughters of Eve (who benefit from it as well). Once the call has been sent, it's just a matter of speaking in a language that the receiver understands. The easiest, most universal language, is, of course, love. But, more on that later on.

Its one thing to be told about magical living, and it's another to see it demonstrated in the life of someone you love and trust. Magic is infectious, and it spreads, touching all the lives that intersect with the life of the practicing witch.

Part One Recap

- Desire to practice is the most important element, and is available to all. The novice who practices is the happiest witch.

- Other stuff from intro chapter

- Use formatting to show importance of recap section
- Stuff. Highpoints. Key elements. What were the principles from the introduction?

Getting down to business: Using the handbook

Become the witch who has it all, by learning how to use the book that explains how to use the most essential tool: magic.

Now that you've begun to understand what we're talking about when we talk about The Modern Witch, and you've had some time to discover if you are, in fact, a joint possessor of the magical heritage, it's time for you to learn how to use the handbook. While it may be read cover-to-cover, like any other book (which is recommended, at least the first time through), understand that the remainder of the handbook is divided into three sections: physical reality, mental reality, and spiritual reality. Use the handbook much as you would a pocket style manual for writing papers: take what you want, as you want for assistance in a particular area. While the handbook works together as a whole, it also serves practically, in the sense that there is a practice for every concern. You could think of it in terms of a macro narrative (the whole book, which demonstrates a whole picture) built from overlapping, harmonious micro narratives (each individual segment within the larger narrative). The three major sections that follow work together to form, and inform, the witch's Reality,[18] and for greatest success, and swiftest route to adept status, the three phases (physical reality, mental reality, and spiritual reality) must be maintained in balance with reference to each other.

1. Most basically, physical reality represents the "shared" reality we have with all other persons, whether they be magically gifted or otherwise. It is in this reality where we practice, occupy ourselves, and engage with others. It is cornerstone, and the witch's careful attention to physical reality is just as important as attention to spiritual reality.

---

[18] The witch has the power to create her own reality; the physical reality in which she lives is subject to the laws of the universe, and the witch who attempts to break these laws will soon find herself disappointed. If you are determined to break the natural laws, it is recommended that you take up fiction writing, or filmmaking.

2. Spiritual reality is truly the most "real" reality. It is the part of the witch that is unseen, most fundamental. Whether it is called a spirit, a soul, or energy, it is the driving force behind everything that is seen in physical reality. It's the place where all things that we see originates. Spiritual reality is addressed in the third section of the handbook, because the way to connect to the spiritual reality is *through the mind.*

3. Mental reality is the in-between world. It is how the spiritual reality connects to the physical reality, and the mind is the tool we use to translate what we see in the spiritual into the physical reality. It's the area where we, as beings of two worlds, come together as one. Spirit and body become whole as they are tied together by the mind.

In each section, we will address the major areas of importance for the direction of the energetic flow of magic. Together, as a whole, these practices harmoniously intertwine into magical living: which is, basically, the living of your absolute best life. Good luck!

Part Two: Physical Reality

There are many ways in which the novice may stay connected effectively to physical reality, which is important especially after she begins actively harnessing the flow of magic, which may tend to attract her attention towards her mental and spiritual sides—balance is of key importance, and since the physical realm is the one which we most obviously share with others, some time and attention will be directed here.

We stay connected to physical reality by learning to listen to the body, and to give it our balanced attention: food, exercise, sleep, sex, outdoor activities, and interactions with people and animals all serve to tie us to physical reality.

The obvious danger is focusing the attention on the physical (whether it be food, exercise, or otherwise) to the neglect of the mental and spiritual aspects of the self, magical or otherwise.

Understanding the basic Order of operations for Magical Living will greatly assist the novice if she will actively put the orders into practice. The sooner, the better!

1. Think

2. Breathe

3. Sleep (when profitable)

4. Drink water (")

5. Eat food (")

6. Secure shelter

7. Secure and wear clothing

- For the above to be pleasant, there should also be present the highest forms/ideals of value: love in all its varieties[19], hope, abundance, et cetera.

Do we remind ourselves to breathe? No. do we remind ourselves to think? No. it's always happening, and it is what sustains life. "*I*

---

[19] Cross-reference to Greek words & descriptions for "love."

think therefore I am.[20]*"* The thoughts within the brain determine the quality and level of life lived. When the novice first begins to understand this, she has begun the most wonderful journey of her life! Magical living is a gift and a pleasure, and with practice, comes easily.

While it is true that we do not require any reminder or *conscious thought* to breathe, we do *benefit* from the art of practiced, controlled breathing. It's useful for stress reduction, peace of mind, and overall wellness. Such is the mind: we think whether we do it consciously or not; it is much better if the novice learn to train her brain to think thoughts that support and harmonize with magical living! In the section on "Summoning" the novice will learn exactly how to do this, however, as a "quick-start," for the enthusiastic novice, I recommend that the novice begin to make herself aware of the order of priority of operations—the list begins with thinking, *then* follows breathing, sleeping, water, food, and so on, for the optimal sustainment of magical living. (Should this be over near "summoning," or is it okay here?)

Generating Reality: Using magic in daily Life

As magically gifted persons, we are *always* using energy. We do this either actively, or passively. Regardless of which way it's used, energy is flowing out from the witch at all times. This is important to be aware of, because, the novice, when beginning to think about and learn how to practice, May, at some point, say to herself, *"that sounds hard."* And if she thinks of it like that, then it will be. However, it's quite liberating to realize that energy is going out whether or not we pay attention to where that energy goes! At first, this notion might be a little scary, but once the novice accustoms herself to the truth of it, she is empowered to use her energy well. To use it to benefit herself, and by extension, the people and community around herself.

Even the adept witch will find that she continuously readjusts her flow of energy; this is just a natural part of the process, and it takes practice. Begin to use your energetic potential—apply it to something that makes you feel good! Crossover into what really is a new reality. It's a higher reality, and I promise you, you will like being there; I can say this with confidence, because the new reality that you enter is a reality of your own creation. I recommend, use your imagination, and

---

[20] cite

make it really good. It will be whatever you decide that you want it to be. It is a continuous process, magical living; it's important, too, to remember that it is a *process.* It is a continuous practice.

It cannot be emphasized enough: Begin *at once* to practice magical living. Begin wherever you are at, whatever you are doing. Baby steps are okay, and highly recommended. A reality that alters too quickly is uncomfortable to adjust to, and for some will be unsustainable. Time is the magic energy exchange that adjusts our minds to the altered reality inherent in magical living. Be grateful for it, and it will serve you well (as will all energy, when you practice directing it). When you begin practicing, you will be astonished at the results that begin to appear in your life, and if you start too soon with giant leaps, you are in danger of losing touch with physical reality (not recommended in the novice stage of practice).

Which is, essentially, the art of *creating the reality in which you live.* Allow me to adjust the lighting, for just a moment, while we talk what we mean when we talk about reality.

Tested with reason, 001

We often claim that a physical object is more real than an object in the mind. For your instruction, I inform you that I possess, on our patio, a beautiful jasmine shrub, which I fully expect to develop fragrant blooms. Novice, can you picture our jasmine? Perhaps some are able, and perhaps others are not able to do so. But I assure you, that jasmine is real. Now, take a moment and think on the Disney character Jasmine. Picture her in your mind? Do you see her? We say that she is *not real,* however, an entire generation of persons, around the world, are able to picture, with accuracy, the appearance of the animated female character. She is real in our minds, and when we talk about her, we all picture the same thing, or very close to the same thing, no matter what part of the world you may be from, or your age, or your personal beliefs about reality. When we think about her, she is more real, in that moment, than the jasmine shrub happily growing on our sunny patio.

You may begin to practice the moment you realize that you are the recipient of a magical heritage, or simply decide to practice because you understand the powerful benefit of doing so. Begin practice immediately, you though you may not feel "qualified," or ready. The key to beginning is *action*.

The witch is *success conscious* in every action she undertakes to perform. There is no distinction between "mundane" and "important" actions. Begin with the small things, because magic happens, especially at first when we are learning to wield it, during the in-between moments. The adept witch understands that whatever she undertakes to do, she does well, regardless of the *surface value*. Small things become big things, and the novice who does the small things well, will evolve into an adept witch who does big things well. Practice! Practice! Practice!

Even the best climbers train before they climb Everest. Train your mind, and the fulfillment of your desires will follow.

Practice, practice, practice!

The important lesson here is that practicing perfection permeates every aspect of the daily existence, continuously, of those who live magically (see "Perfection," p._). As the novice practices, she may, throughout that practice, experience minor setbacks—interruptions may occur, and they may seem insurmountable. However, as any dedicated climber will tell you, even the most terrifying peaks are surmountable, if the climber is well-prepared for them.

Celebrate the small victories, and prepare yourself to celebrate larger and larger victories.

Overcoming practical obstacles

Negative emotions have no place in magical living, except as a pinch to remind the novice that she is, in fact, in charge; the key to success in all of the areas detailed in the following sections is to *first* practice the habit of mastering your emotional state—creating a positive reality in which all the pleasant and beneficial aspects of witchcraft may be enjoyed[21]. Here is a wonderful opportunity for the

---

[21] Cross-reference to summoning section

novice: any perceived setback or failure may be viewed as reminders to "keep awake," and also as reminders that perhaps something bigger and even better is on the way—maintain this attitude, and good things will be continuously attracted to you.

Learn to trust your gut. Then learn to adjust it.

When you feel bad, for whatever reason, that generates and attracts more of the same type of energy. Instead, shift your focus (this becomes easy with practice) onto something that makes you feel good. A happy hope or dream for the future, anything that the witch has that she loves—it can be as mundane as a comfortable favorite pair of shoes, an animal, or a friend. All that matters is the feeling, which will draw to itself more of that same feeling.

Harnessing the power that generates magical living is wonderfully easy, and may be practiced and mastered by any determined person, with or without magical heritage; however, your will be required to overcome the following negative emotions, and to overcome them continuously, throughout the waking day. They are sometimes recognized under the following names:

1. Distraction

2. disbelief

3. fear

4. worry

There are many other names, but the feelings that they impart are the same. Are they good? No. If the novice finds that she is "not sure" how she feels about something, it may be that she uses more time to decide on a thing. However, it is worth noting that decisions made instinctively and quickly (exercising good judgment) tend to be the decisions the witch is most comfortable with later on.

Overcoming these, and any negative, contradictory feelings, is as simple as putting them out of your mind through habits which you may integrate into your life at any time you choose (see "mindfulness," p._)

If you're not sure how you feel about something, check yourself. *You always know when you feel good.*

It is an active choice, but it's as simple as a shift in the mind, and may begin as easily as saying, *"I can change our mind."*

(Attn.)

As we continue, We will point out a useful fact for the novice—specifically, that *Innocence and purity* are exactly opposite of shame and guilt, two of the root causes of *worry*, which is a common assailant of magical practice. As you begin to practice magical living, you may feel *worried* that it won't work for you, or that you're efforts are "not good enough" or you may feel ashamed that it seems too hard to practice. whatever your particular worry may be, you will Easily conquer all worry with a spirit of childlike wonder and delight—with innocence of heart and purity of thought—you're doing a great job, and tell yourself this!

The novice must, regardless of the circumstances or events, or actions that she has experienced or participated in in the past, *practice* living with innocence and purity. This is done simply: only do the things that you feel good about. Do things, participate in things, say, think, and write the things that you're comfortable with everyone you know reading, seeing, or being aware of. Be comfortable doing what you do in full light. Conduct yourself well, and you will be blameless, regardless what you do. If you do it well, and you cause no harm, then you have effectively freed yourself from all criticism and judgment[22]. Conduct yourself, always, as if you will give a reporting of your actions; which is what you are doing—you are reporting to yourself!

Maintaining Physical Health

Health begins as an important state of mind. The body of the witch is her sacred temple, and it is the physical manifestation of her spirit into the visible realm. What the witch thinks of herself is what is manifested for all to see. As the physical container in which her mind (soul/spirit/energy) is at home, the temple will serve as an accurate reflection of the mind within. Much as the home (apartment, house, condo, et cetera) is the physical manifestation and reflection of the

---

[22] The editor mentions this since the powerful witch may find herself drawn to unusual occupations, activities, experiences, and people.

34

witch that dwells within it, so is the flesh to the mind of the witch. Care for your temple; it will inform you of any requirements.

So the mind, also the body.

The witch draws to herself the state of health, and it is in this ideal state the witch, mind and body, will thrive. The best practice for health and wellness is simple, and begins with the reduction and removal of stressors from the daily life and interpersonal relationships[23] .This is done through careful attention of the thought processes of the witch, and thought processes of the companions she keeps company with. It benefits the witch to attract and maintain companions that radiate health, as an indicator of the health of the mind[24].

The body is the animal part of the witch, the mind serves as the connecting link to the spiritual part. The body serves as host to the mind, and it desires to be worthy of the mind within. By embracing the freedom of magical living, the body will begin to tell the witch exactly what it desires. It is worthy of trust. In Learning to listen to, and obey, the simple requirements of the body, the witch will be delighted with the results.

Beauty (add more specific advice in this section, basic stuff that We do)

Beauty, as a ritual, goes beyond the common practice of hair, makeup, skin-care, and style. It is a holistic process, and each part of the ritual bears importance, as the whole is only as powerful as the weakest element. Fitness is a component of the Beauty ritual, providing a firm foundation for the remaining rituals, and is, alongside diet, the foundation for physical beauty in the witch (which, remember, accounts for fully 1/3 of the witch's identity, and must not be ignored). Lucky for the magically inclined, they are lovers of movement and nature, and "getting exercise" is easy and pleasurable. Since she dedicates time to listening and responding to the requirements of her body, she is able to meet her fitness requirements in this way as well.

The ritual of putting on lotion

By taking the time to apply lotion to the skin, at whatever time it pleases her to do so, the novice has a wonderful

---

[23] Cross-reference to relationships

[24] Are you concerned about the health of your mind? welcome to the most delightful catch 22 in psychology. You have an unusually firm grip on reality.

opportunity to take inventory of herself. Not unlike the way the groom takes note of the horse as it prepares before a ride—hands run all over the body, smoothing down the muscles, feeling for any bumps or irregularities, and finding an object, ultimately, praiseworthy. The witch lives mostly in her mind, constantly aware of the flow of magic in and through her, so the ritual of lotion helps her to remember that she is also present in the shared plane of reality, one where aches and pains will build up if she ignores this fact. Regular visits to the body will preserve youth and most basic, essential, physical beauty.

Hair and Cosmetics[25] preferences range, from witch to witch, and follow their own rules. However, they do follow common practice (CP), and tend to be uncommonly good examples within the parameters of CP.

Hygiene approaches obsession for the modern witch, who will practice her stringent standards, without regard to company. What this manifests as might include: carrying an oral care kit, hairbrush, handy-wipes, et cetera, in her handbag or purse. Her hygiene items are never far from reach. The bathing routine is similar to the sleep routine: it depends entirely on what the body requires. Hair will be

---

[25] The editor advises that you learn to ask yourself important questions, such as, "can i get into the packaging which our cosmetics are contained?" if the answer is "no," then perhaps those cosmetics had best stay in their packaging. Chanel provides an excellent system for self-checks in their packaging. The foundations are easy to get into, they blend easily, even on naked skin. They apply perfectly, every time. The blush is a little more challenging to get into, and that provides a check point—should we be applying blush, or should we return to the party and feel satisfied that our makeup is already perfect? Lipsticks are a whole new world—the reds are encased in a complicated two-step system. The packaging screams at the user, "use me with care!" Apply with discretion. You'll look great when you do. If cosmetics are difficult and time consuming to apply, then there are underlying concerns for the witch to address. (Add these footnotes to above text)

washed with frequency determined by the witch, and the shower frequency ranges, though usually between 1-3 times per day.

(Expand fitness routine and beauty advice, add practical applications)

Daily Routine: About the House

Rising and preparing for the day

At What time, and in what way does the witch awake to face her day? She awakes when her body wills, and she does so happily, content and satisfied from peaceful, recuperative slumber[26]. What are of *absolute importance* are the amount and the quality of the sleep achieved. The witch must neither sleep too little, or too much. She will learn to listen to, and obey, her body and its requirements, with practice. The body is supremely adaptable, and will use well this, or any other freedom. With practice, trusting the body will become one of the easiest, most pleasant ways to maintain good health. Again let us repeat: the body may, and ought to be, trusted.

Practical Application, 001/Tested Empirically, 001

Sleep is useful for beauty, and it is restorative, if it is the *right kind of sleep.* Sleep is meant to be a pleasant, recuperative, healing time when the body takes the lessons learned during the day, and then *practices them in the imagination.* It may be helpful to the witch to learn the art of *lucid dreaming*, so that she may actively practice in her sleep (flying is delightful, and we recommend it). Basically, and most practically, the suggestions that the novice makes to her mind during the day (through the useful practice of the incantations (p._).), have the ability to come alive and be practiced during the sleep-time. Sleep is when we practice what we have been "teaching" our subconscious mind during the day; it is best if this is an active practice, since we train our subconscious mind regardless of whether we do it intentionally; the thoughts that we think during the day become our dreams at night. It is our testing ground for new

---

[26] While this is true, the editor will confess to using less sleep over time, both staying up late and rising reasonably early, thought happily punctuating the day with naps, when desired.

realities, new thoughts, revelations, and ideas. Why do we only sometimes remember our dreams? When we discover the answer, we will happily reveal it. Now there is some argument as to which is "real" life, and "waking" life, and if they are one in the same. The aboriginal peoples in both Australia and South Africa talk about the "dreamtime," which posits an interesting theory on the topic, but we will examine that shortly.

We wake up better each time we wake.

Cosmetics and physical beauty

The witch understands well the fact that she is a person in three realms: the body, the spirit, and the mind, which connects the two. If she learns to actively employ her mind, she may remain balanced between the physical and the spiritual world—an ideal state of balance which will benefit the novice in practice. Part of this truth is revealed in physical beauty, and we mean the most basic kind.

tested with reason, 001

While every witch looks vastly different from every other, it remains true that basic physical beauty is available to *all who practice magic.* While it is the most basic, it is also the most important, and lasting variety of physical beauty: health and wellness. Living well demonstrates itself in the body the same way that an apple hanging from a limb demonstrates an apple tree—we may, for ease of understanding, suggest that the witch is like the fruit tree: most of who she is may be seen, but not easily identified until she begins bearing fruit. Then all will know exactly what type of tree she is—whether apple, pear, orange, or some strange new variety—it will be clear what she is as soon as the fruit grows.

People will either admire that fruit, and pluck it fresh and at its best (or even a little early, if you like some tartness!), or it will become over-ripened, and fall from the tree to rot below. Such a sad fate!

Our bodies are part of the "fruit" we show in the visible realm, and those bodies tell part of the story of who we are. Not the whole story, but part. It's important to remember that neglect of either will be to the detriment of the magically gifted. So, pay attention to your fruit; and if you are a pear, then be the choicest pear. And if you are an apple, be the choicest apple. The tree who tries to bear pecans when it is a hazelnut, will be disappointed (unless there is a hybrid, which is becoming more and more common in our fruits).

Varying degrees of symmetry exist between magical and non-magical alike, but the most beautiful all have the same things in common:

- healthy, glowing skin

- correct posture and flexibility of movement

- an appropriate weight for their height, age, athleticism, and bone-structure

- well-maintained hair

- healthy, clean mouth (teeth and breath)

- Well-cut clothing made in quality fabrics.

- A lifestyle which includes both aerobic and anaerobic activities

Sleep, when done properly, will serve the purpose of allowing the novice to wake up *better* each time she does so. Neglecting the importance and quality of sleep (quality is key, length may vary) is as unpleasant as the neglect of water. And we know, with good authority, that neglecting the intake of clean, fresh, water, is dangerous for the body of the novice as well as her familiar!

Practical application, 001

Let us talk a moment about essentials for sustenance of life. We frequently think of them in terms of what we can see, and we think of them in, what we believe are, orders of importance. For example, it is frequently accepted that a person cannon go without food, and we can see all of our "food," if we have eyes. However, the human, whether a daughter of Eve, or a descendants of the Watchers (footnote to historical origin story in appendix), can go without food for quite some time (footnote, it has been our habit over the years to fast for the period of cleansing the body, usually 5-7 days, but as many as 30 days). She cannot, however, go without water for more than a few days—possibly up to seven, but a medical authority should be consulted before tempting any such fast! We know from scientific research, sad, sad research[27], yet very useful, that a cat can only survive for about three days without *sleep*. Sleep deprivation is one of the vilest forms of torture. But we see water, and we see how we look when we sleep, either through pictures, or someone else's description of how we looked. There is empirical evidence. Do we "see" air with our eyes? No. we see *evidences*, such as clouds, or colors in the sunset. The gas-mixture that we breathe, that sustains life, unseen to the naked human eye, no matter the magical lineage status. We can go a very short time without out good, clean air to breathe. We trust that it contains oxygen, and that it contains nitrogen (up to 70%), we take on good faith that nitrogen is present in our atmosphere—but we take it as a matter of course, because *we would all die right quick without it.* And it is a thing we cannot see.

Like a list of priorities throughout the day such as "get dressed" and "shower," the obvious we remember, because you know that it is better to put fresh clothes on after getting out of the shower. So, air is more vital for life than sleep, and sleep more than water, and water more than food, and food more than shelter, and so on. So, it would suggest that maybe, the things that we cannot see (thankfully! Can you imagine looking through a fog of molecules all the time! Our goodness gracious!) Are, in fact, the *most vitally important.*

Have courage! Wake up! You're better each time you do.

Transplant *understanding.*

(Side jaunt—is faith enough, without understanding? Depends whether you want religion, or renaissance.)

Upon waking, the witch will first take inventory of, and prioritize, her priorities. The check for missed communication transmissions (texts, email, phone messages, blog comments, et cetera) that occurred during the night, is generally followed by the first trip to the toilet; the witch understands the importance of natural evacuation, and does so easily and frequently. During this process, the witch may take time to meditate, and

A mirror helps you to see, and correct, your flaws. Fix your face, and be kind to what you see in the mirror.

---

[27] Reference to cat sleep deprivation study (water study).

clear her mind, to prepare it for the day ahead. She may also check her feelings, examine those feelings, and make any necessary adjustments to those feelings, setting herself in the right state of *mind* to face all that is delivered during the day[28]. Practice is easy, and the more frequently the novice practices, the more quickly she achieves adept status—the point at which the witch evolves from having *magic moments* in her daily life, to living *magically.*

Inside the Home

The witch's home is an intimate sanctuary, and one of physical manifestations of how the witch thinks about herself, and of how she

cares for her mind. To be invited inside the witch's home, and experience the witch's hospitality, is one of the highest honors she might bestow on any person. For some, her home is a perfect haven, peaceful, balanced, and beautiful. Welcome guests will experience calm and a sense of peace in the home, and will desire to return to it (if they can find it[29]). While for others, it may be a den of heartache and perceived loss[30]. What is allowed to enter the home will meet exacting standards, and what is permitted to *remain* in the home does so by demonstrating beauty, utility, spiritual, or entertainment value. The home will

The witch's home may also be hell: an exaggerated reminder of past failures, and prophet of future defeat. Be careful about your house!

be consistently purged of unnecessary objects (or persons). No item is

---

[28] Practice, witch—you will be tested! You receive *only what you ask for*, and if what you receive is unpleasant, than know that it is merely the result of old patterns of thought. Think about ordering something impulsively online, the forgetting about it. When it arrives, you may not want it, nonetheless, it arrived *because you ordered it.*

Even subconscious thought counts, thus the importance of practicing the art of training the subconscious (see "subconscious," p._)

[29] The home of a witch may be difficult for the non-magical to find, even if they have been to the home on multiple occasions. Why is this true? That's for someone smarter than your editor to answer. empirical evidence suggests the accuracy of the claim. Regardless of the quality of the directions or GPS system, or the seeming ease and convenience of location, the witch's home is difficult to find.

[30] For, can we lose what wasn't ours to begin with? (see "*seduction,* 'p._).

safe from purging, but objects brought in are given fair trial-period, and some objects may become part of the *home*. The closet is an area of frequent purges, though the novice will most likely refine her closet to perfection in a short period of time after waking to her magical gift.

The witch who takes *care* with herself, feels good about herself. This truth manifests itself in every area of her life, and is particularly evident in the appearance and atmosphere of her home. This care she takes with herself is extended to those blessed souls invited into her home. There will be no flurry of activity upon the arrival of the guest; the home is always ready to receive guests and deliver hospitality, because the witch treats herself, first, to her own good hospitality.

Home Décor & Energy Loops

The décor in the home of the witch is peaceful, purposeful, and meaningful—though this will mean something different to each witch. The home should inspire and comfort the witch who dwells within, and there are small actions that the novice may perform to transform her residence into a powerfully positive place of residence. A few details are essential: there must be elements to represent key ancestors (particularly ancestral witches) either in photographs or other physical element; this small gesture serves as gentle reminder of the heritage from which she has received her magical gift. She is a possessor and transformer of great power, it is her birthright, and she is grateful to remember those ancestors who prepared the way for her. The witch may, it should be notes, pass along her magical gift, if she chooses, in at least two ways: either through her offspring, or through some creative outlet which causes an "awakening" in a slumbering fellow witch (or witches).

In addition to art and other wall-hangings, the *mirror* is as vital to the witch's home as is water to the fish's home.

Why is this so?

The mirror seems to be an integral part of the witch's repertoire, and this has been historically demonstrated to be true. Mirrors are magical devices, used in all manner of summoning, by ourriad magical creatures or practitioners. They are powerful even in their simplest use, and the novice who learns how to use the mirror will benefit from doing so.

The novice must, first, learn to look in the mirror and be kind to what she sees. The mirror is an opportunity: use the mirror when you practice or daydream—it gives you a supportive, honest, believer as audience. If you believe in yourself first, others will follow. And belief can come from the tiniest seed: Practice will deliver all of the belief you will require.

Practice with or without an audience; it matters not who watches, only that you practice.

Surrounding the home with mirrors also serves the purpose of reflecting the witch's feelings about herself onto those who enter her home. Guests will perceive the witch, while in her home, as she sees herself. Her feelings about herself are reflected on them, and this is an opportunity for a positive energy feedback loop. Ideally, guests will be caught up in the energetic feeling that "life is good, and we am happy to be here in this moment," which is a *good feeling* for both the witch who sets the tone, and for the guest who experiences the feedback loop. How comfortable the novice is with guests inside her residence is a good indicator of how comfortable she is with herself. If, novice, you are uncomfortable inviting guests into your home, embrace the opportunity before you! Make those necessary adjustments that will bring about that delightful positive energetic feedback loop.

Generating Positive Energy Loops in the Home

The home is a sacred place, and the witch knows this well. Here are a few basic suggestions for creating a positive, harmonious energetic feedback loop in the home

1. Remove distracting clutter, whether paperwork (buy a filing box, or use old shoe boxes for organization and storage), dishes in the kitchen, or keys and other essentials. *A place for everything, and everything in its place.* Clear out all chaotic elements as your first priority.

2. Keep clothing where it belongs: dirty clothing in the hamper, out of the way, and clean clothing folded or hung. Clothing strewn about will cause distress in even the most adept witch.

3. Adjust the lighting. The home should be well-lit, but not overly bright. We highly recommend the use of multiple lamps or wall-sconces, as a preference over any over-head light. Neon, fluorescent, or high-wattage ought to be avoided.

4. Airflow. The use of fans, whether ceiling or otherwise, will cause continuous airflow throughout the home, and this circulation has a positive effect on the witch and her familiars.

5. Natural elements present: maintain in the home representative elements, such as wood, water, earth, and metal (also fire from the lighting, circulating air from fans). Living plants are recommended, bamboo and cacti are easy to start with for the novice without the green thumb.

6. Wall color, wall hangings, and furniture. Use color to change the way each room *feels* to you; trust your instincts on this, and play with different options. Consult an expert if it pleases you to do so. If you rent your home, wall color options may be limited, but you certainly are able to adjust your wall hangings. Images that feel peaceful, and reflect the feelings you want to experience should be used as preference. If the art on your walls is your own, be sure that such art reflects what you want to experience.

7. Furniture. Beware negative energy and dead space. Furniture need not be jammed against the walls; courageously try new options, and adjust the arrangement until it feels right. The goals of the individual witch are reflected in her arrangement of furniture. For

example, in our home, the den area has been arranged with the specific goal of generating harmonious conversation between several persons—the furniture placement reflects this. Each individual may comfortably sit in any position and be a comfortable distance looking towards any other seated person, without craning the neck or twisting the body. Balance is the most important element in the arrangement of furniture, and you will *feel* it intuitively when it is right for you.

8. Photos. Display photos of yourself with friends and family in your happiest moments—see yourself at your best.

9. Sound. Find balance between sound and silence, and when you use sound in the home, use sound and music that is peaceful, or uplifting, or... whatever you desire to feel. Music has a profound ability to affect mood, and should be used judiciously.

10. Fragrance. Candles, incense, air fresheners all have their place, but the most important thing is that the home be, first, clean. Clean, and well-ventilated spaces are of utmost priority for wellness, followed by additional pleasing aromas. The use of fragrance in the home serves to uplift, when used appropriately (rather than to "cover up" foul odors).

It is the "empty" spaces that we create inside the home which we actually use: the solid door, but the emptiness which we pass through, the arrangement of furniture, but our bodies move around that furniture and through the space between. Mindful of the *in-between*, we create the opportunity for harmonious balance in the décor of the home.

In addition to the mirrors throughout the home, the décor creates and sustains the energy feedback loop when the witch outside the home. While she is within the home, her energy can, and does, dictate the nature of the atmosphere and environment—which is what she will come home to (the energy generated in her absence). When the witch learns to create a positive energy feedback loop through placement of the mirrors and other décor in the home, she will be greeted by a forceful flow of positive energy whenever she returns to the home, which acts to accelerate the upward momentum of the energy all around (energy sources joining together at the same pace and going in the same direction: increased velocity).

If the thought of returning to your home puts a damper on your mood, start with adjusting the décor; even if it's just a shift of the furniture[31]. Let me also recommend that the novice learn to become comfortable with the mirror, and to do so speedily. Like any of the other practices, repetition mingled with good feelings will yield a desirable outcome, *even for the novice who begins with hating what she sees.* It's okay to come back to this later; of greater importance is just to begin where you are. Each lesson will build on every other, and if this seems too difficult at first, it will become easy at a later time.

The Bath.

Is always clean, and is always fully stocked with essentials. There is always enough, and there is always a "spare" for any guests who may require toiletries. The bathroom is an extension of the hospitality of the home, and contains all the comforts that the witch herself, or her guests, may require for the cleanliness and health of the body.

Be fearless of the toilet! It's a place for health and wellness to occur; neglect will result in far-ranging negative effects.

tested empirically, 001

For having no better place to make mention, permit me to interject here with some empirical information. We use the "bath" to clean our bodies, and also to evacuate our bodies of unneeded excess. Since the cleaning of the body is covered quite nicely in all media, let us turn our attention and shine a small light on evacuations. Let us do so with a true story.

A friend and co-worker who we knew for about two years had been suffering, and she had been suffering for a long time. She had many troubles, though she was not in the habit of

---

[31] The editor recommends the useful practice of feng shui.

complaint. However, we did know, from talking with her, that she was unsatisfied with her weight, and this had been a source of trouble for her over a period of years. We listened to what she said, and she told me that she was beginning to see a new health care practitioner. Now, she had seen many doctors over the years, to no avail.

After having visited with the new doctor, she visited with me, and was delighted to have begun to see some positive evidence of this new treatment, and we asked her about it in greater detail. What we found was surprising. She had been put on a nutritional regimen to address the fact that her eliminations were weekly. This young woman told me that she only had an elimination once per week, or maybe once every ten days. We were shocked, and expressed our shock to her. All week long, she would feed her body, and only once per week, eliminate waste? We talked about this at some length. She told me, with sincerity, that she didn't know that was a problem, or that anyone else did it any differently. We confidently shared with her that we have two per day! And naturally, without stimulant aid (just that found present in fibrous foods). When we began to compare notes on our health, it seemed that this factor was the main difference between our habits. She exercised with some regularity, and she ate with moderation. Yet there was a significant difference between the health and fitness of our bodies. Here was an otherwise smart woman, who didn't understand the fundamental importance of natural, regular evacuations. Our body takes the good stuff, the nutrients useful, and tosses out the rest. Removing the excess is important to wellness!

The eliminations and evacuations of the body are also a good analogy for the spirit of the witch: what goes in cycles through, then all of the excess, the unnecessary, is *eliminated.* The novice may feel annoyed with herself for allowing negative energy to flow through her, but she ought to keep in mind: practice putting good energy in, and what will come out the other side is excess positive energy.

The Bedroom.

The most sacred spot inside the witch's home, those who enter here, are advised do so with positive intent. The novice may use the bedroom for any number of activities, but use the bedroom only for sleep (and intimacy), whenever possible. The bedroom should be a peaceful place. If the novice has trouble sleeping in the bedroom, she may be pleased to make energy rearrangements within, such as décor adjustments or changes, or the alteration of the direction of the bed.

Hospitality

Open the door to all who knock, but only invite in what is good. You may engage with any and all on the patio, and do so fearlessly. With grace and magic.

Be polite and pay attention, *first to yourself and then to others.*

By practicing hospitality first on and for herself, by keeping a tidy, well-organized home, well-stocked with pleasantries, others will enjoy the hospitality of the witch as well. The witch, regardless of her intentions, will treat others the way that she treats herself. Good hospitality, to yourself and others, is a cornerstone of good health and healing, because acts of hospitality are both pleasurable, and selfless.

What this means can be broken down into a few basic principles.

1. The basics of hospitality demand that you graciously offer food, water, and shelter to those who ask for it; however, these basics are just the beginning of what is, really, a much deeper and truly spiritual practice. The "traveler" is vulnerable, and the force of hospitality protects the traveler—whether the individual is travelling physically or spiritually.

2. By maintaining an "open" home, you are indicating to the world that you perceive the universe as a friendly place. This sets the tone for yourself and any guests.

3. The gracious entertainment offered by the hostess, by the simple gesture of offering refreshments, breaks boundaries between people, and creates an opportunity for harmonious dialogue, even between persons who share different perspectives.

4. By allowing the "other" in, we expand our own consciousness.

5. Hospitality is the opposite of hostility. One embraces while the other rejects. Check your attitude, and check what your home says about your attitude. Does your home reject visitors? The removal of unfriendly elements will increase the peace and harmony of the home, with or without guests.

6. Practicing hospitality creates an opportunity to practice trust, and the novice who learns to trust is the novice who is surrounded by trustworthy people. "Hospitality' is a practice, but it's also a safe place, in an energetic or metaphysical sense, for pleasant and harmonious bonds between individuals to develop, be those individuals magical or non-magical.

The kitchen is the foundation upon which all hospitality outflow rests. The kitchen will vary to suit the particular desires of each witch, but it must be well-stocked and well appointed. Allow me to reiterate, what this means is particular to the witch[32]. No guest is treated as a "surprise," and should always be greeted as welcome, expected guests.

Tested with Reason, 001

Do you understand that you treat others the way that you treat yourself? Are you patient and kind with yourself? Or are you critical and impatient? Are you demanding and angry? Or are you gentle and peaceful? *Treat yourself the way you wish to treat others.* When we think of the Golden Rule from this perspective, it gives us fresh light to examine how we *really* think and behave. With this exercise comes responsibility, but it is a liberating responsibility. Self-compassion is where it begins; do good by feeling good. Be kind to yourself, first, and all the people around you will enjoy the benefit of your kindness as well. Take the time to take care of yourself.

---

[32] The editor always maintains the following basics in her kitchen: kale, sheep's milk feta, raw almonds, olive oil, honey crisp apples, gouda cheese, and mineral water. A fruit, vegetable, and cheese platter will please almost any guest, regarless of dietary restrictions.

Health, and the physical appearance of the body

The body is the physical manifestation of "you." You, witch are a creature in three parts, as we've begun to discuss: body, mind, spirit.

Tested with Reason, 001

Discussing the physical health of the body presents a wonderful opportunity to become empowered. Whether the novice chooses to perceive time as linear or cyclical, it's important to remember that it moves *forward*, always. Whether it moves forward in a recurring cycle (as suggested by many of the ancients) of from beginning to end (a common belief held by many modern peoples), it always moves *forward.* Beware the common curse, "I'm going to get back to…" whether it's "getting back" to a previously imagined level of physical fitness, health, weight, eating habits, or whatever it is, "getting *back*," will effectively *prevent* forward momentum. Instead, use your words effectively—make every utterance an incantation, and you will be astounded by the magic that surrounds you. First, train your thinking: *move forward* into your ideal self, whether it is moving forward into a state of health, fitness, or any other goal for the physical mind or body. Always moving forward! Let your words reflect this progression. A quick tip for the novice who wishes to change her physical appearance in some way or another: take the time to envision yourself as you wish to be. Instead of placing your focus on what you used to be, or used to look like at some moment in the past, place your focus on your idealized self, and begin to visualize yourself looking and being your ideal *now.* Look at yourself in the mirror (We love mirrors for their wonderful usefulness and applicability), and see yourself, at your present age, and see yourself with the glow of health, at the weight you wish to be. Begin to look for signs and evidences that support this vision of yourself, and you will soon discover that there are more and more signs of this idealized self emerging each day. This ideal self exists already inside you, and very much wants to come out. Shift focus from "getting back," to moving forward, and you will be astonished at how quickly you are able to achieve results. Like any of the other tools in the witch's belt, this takes practice, but practice yields results! We encourage you to begin immediately to put this to the test—we will also tell you that the most difficult part will be convincing your mind; once the mind is trained, through practice, to believe that the process works, the body will happily, easily, and quickly follow suit.

Have you ever said to yourself, "I wish I drank more water"? There is an easy solution to ensuring that your body is getting the water it desires: buy crystal water goblets. Try this, by purchasing just one crystal goblet to drink out of, if you like. Once you experience this, you will understand how simple it is to begin to positively alter the experience of the kitchen. This will change the way that you use and eat food, allowing you to eat it with pleasure, in amounts suitable to the body you wish to dwell in. is the kitchen a place of dread and failure for you, novice? Turn that around! Make it, first, the place where you drink lots of water. This simple action will begin a course-adjustment that will amaze and delight you. Ensuring that the physical body is continuously hydrated (remember, if you're thirsty, you're already dehydrated), you will be delighted to discover that you feel "hungry" less frequently. And when you do feel the pangs of hunger, you can deal with them in a respectful way—by eating healthful, satisfying food in an amount appropriate for the body you wish you possess. Eat for the body you want!

A well-appointed kitchen will change the way you use your entire home, a vast source of positive energetic power (magic).

On food and eating

Food is either medicine or poison.

A little poison now and again is pleasurable, and we would be so bold as to recommend it. However, as a practice, we also recommend that the novice and adept alike consume medicinal food. This is the food that heals your body, and provides the stable house in which your mind lives. The body has requirements, and they are simple. Keep the dietary regimen simple, punctuated only occasionally with more elaborate eating, and the body will adjust itself to whatever its baseline state is. Generally, this will be some slight variation on the body in its immediately post-pubescent state. It will be youthful, healthful, and able to move freely and flexibly to adapt to everyday scenarios. Basic strength training is healthful, and may be accomplished using just the weight of the body---a gym, trainer, or equipment is not required, although some novices may choose to employ the services of such resources, in which case we say, "do what seems best to you!" in any case, the easiest and sufficiently profitable method of attaining exercise is to simply use your body for the purposes which is was designed to function: lifting, bending, walking interspersed with running, dancing, jumping, climbing, and so on. All of the activities that engaged the play time of childhood are more than sufficient for the basic maintenance of the health of the physical body.

The novice practices a variety of magic that is extraordinarily practical and useful in applicable terms. That is, while there are archaic magics available to the witch (such as summoning and generating reality), the majority of the magic performed by the witch is most simply the living of the well-rounded, excellent life. A healthy body, a healthy mind, healthy relationships, these are all evidences of magical living, not, as some may have been led to believe, the keeping of cats, brooms, and sacrificial offerings. While familiars remain important, the rest of the stereotypical evidences are the irrelevant accoutrements of earlier times.

How to cut your own hair
> (add illustrated 1page each long hair, short hair, bangs, plus split-end treatment, etc)

An evening at home, or out

How the modern witch entertains herself might be unusual to the non-magical person: she may find it challenging to "shut off" or, continuously desiring to engage only in such actions that give direct pleasure or benefit—and her idea of pleasure and benefit are individually defined, though usually very specific.

The witch is jealous of her time, understanding well the time/energy exchange[33]. How she spends her energy will vary from witch to witch, but it is common to find that the witch spends much of the *in-between* focusing her energy on personal pursuits and practices. She is a purposeful creature by habit, and her idea of *fun* might be unusual—such as learning a foreign language, or the cuisine of another region or country.

---

[33] Cross-reference to time/energy section

An evening at home might include cooking, writing, reading, researching, planning, special beauty treatments, practice of any of the arts, or even television or film viewing. The practicing novice *has become comfortable in her own company*, and uses her energy effectively, whether its industry or leisure, an evening at home is a pleasure.

An evening out might include a date with a friend or (potential) lover, dining, visual or audio entertainment (a movie or a musical performance); some enjoy bar-hopping. Novices might notice that they slowly become more jealous of their "time", precious and powerful as each moment has the potential to be; however, it is important to "get out" periodically, and to use such experiences to hit the "reset" button. This practice also may serve as the metaphorical *pinch* to remind the novice that she is, in fact, awake and in control of her own destiny. Continuously re-setting ensures that you stay on your chosen path (or in your tractor beam), and entertainment and companionship (or romance) can help to keep the enthusiastically practicing novice grounded in the reality we all share. Anyone with a working knowledge of energy (such as electricity) understands well the value of *grounding.*

The Close of Day

Regardless of what occupied the novice prior to the time the witch submits to slumber, she will perform the evening rituals (varying depending on the witch). Regardless of what those rituals may be, neglect of these rituals will result in bad feeling, and because of this, she rarely neglects them. Such rituals generally contain cleanliness activities, cosmetics removal, clothing change or removal, and a beverage, a book, or a period of focused reflection. The ritual informs the body that it is "sleep time," and gives it a few moments to accept the order and respond accordingly. While it is a form of magic, this shutting down of the senses to outside stimuli requires, for sleep to be beneficial, a getting into the right state of mind—this will preclude the most useful, healing sleep.

Planning the Perfect Day, every day

"All I know is that it comes."

By taking a few moments at the start of each day to visualize what will occur during the day (plans, errands, chores, expectations, and so on), and making a habit of doing so, the novice begins to take charge of her reality. By planning for what she wants to happen, and focusing on the desired outcome, she sets *plans* for success. Remember—what the witch visualizes and plans for, she gets.

Visualize: make "short films" in your mind in advance of all your actions. See your desired outcome as *already happened*. Watch the instant replay in your imagination. In this way, create the perfect day, every day.

By deciding what she wants, and planning for it, the novice honors the flow of magical energy which flows through her. And this energy[34] honors her requests. Failure threatens, and occasionally temporary setbacks occur.

By shaping the mind, and the daily life, through the practice of visualizing the events of the day at its start, the witch begins to permit her desires to come true. It's a stepped process, and one that the novice practices continuously, without ceasing (part of the responsibility of magical living); because it is so important, elements of the process will be oft repeated throughout the handbook. The more of the steps the novice becomes adept at, the more quickly she will begin to see results of the energy exchanged (energy in, results out). As introduction and overview, let us begin here:

Practical application, 001 (fix title later)

- **Decide** what you want, and be very clear (in your own mind) about

  what that is. Prepare your mind to receive the things you desire:

  practice daydreaming (see also mindfulness and imagination, p._).

---

[34] Which, in this case, is synonomous with the concept "time."

Even if it's as small as completing a household project, or even acquiring breakfast. Daydreams are the previews of things to come[35] , and being in the habit of balancing immediate desires with larger desires will assist he novice in using her energy wisely.

- **Payment** is required for the delivery of *every desire*, and for everything that exists, there is an energetic opposite. The witch must submit payment for what you desire, but the good news is that each witch gets to decide what that payment is! The wonderful news is that we may pay with a currency of our own choosing; we highly recommend paying with renewable resources (such as the fruit of some talent or creativity, alongside the practice of genuine gratitude).

- **Honor** the magical flow of energy: Include a *time-frame*[36] for the completion/receipt of this thing. Time, as we will repeat throughout the text, is kind to those who demonstrate respect. Name a specific date for completion, or use the *present tense* as your time constraint.

  Begin at once in your plan, and note the beginning in your calendar; simply accept that you are, in fact, ready, and any additional belief required will follow, if you *practice believing for whatever you are planning* (calling, see "summoning, p._").

---

[35] "Imagination is everything. It is the preview of life's coming attractions." Albert Einstein.

[36] The "time-frame" is set by the witch, and is *how long*, or *how much energy* exchange *she requires* to align her state of mind to the idea that she may have what she has requested. All "time" is, in this instance, is the witch preparing her mind to receive whatever outcome she desires. She may think that she ought to do this or that, before receiving, and so, if she believes that, "this or that" must be done before her mind is ready to accept that she can have what she wants. It's energy exchange, pure and simple, and we will discuss this more later.

- **Write and recite.** There is power in the word, whether that word (or words) is written down or spoken aloud. Combine both for most effectual use of the tool. By writing down what she wants, (in the calendar, on the list, and wherever else you'll see it daily), the payment she is willing to submit (the energy the witch expects to expend in exchange for the delivery of the witch's desires). The witch will benefit from the daily recitation aloud, and following that up with rewriting, or re-clarifying, until her request is *exactly* what she desires. This is part of the summoning process, and the training of the subconscious mind (cross reference to both).

- **Realize.** When you have a true understanding of what you really want, then this process will result in the "realizing" of dreams. The dream become reality; the witch realizes that *she can have* what she desires.

Realization is the result of one of the following energy exchanges: *The formula works*[37]: the method of exchange that is implemented belongs to the witch to choose, and each method has its own pleasures and rewards.

Regardless of which method of exchange chosen by the witch, the point is only that the witch choose *to believe in a future where she gets to live out all of her highest hopes and deepest desires.* The future where the witch secures the starring role in the greatest story she can imagine: her own personal "greatest story ever told."

We cannot emphasize enough the importance of the above ideas; the secret dreams, the ones the witch may or may never have shared with anyone else—the ones that seem *too good* to become reality— imagine what that would look like. She must develop, or recapture, the ability and habit of dreaming, and to dream that she is the star of the best show *she ever saw.* There are great stories throughout history, the great ourths, traditions, folk tales, hero stories, and the romances (as seen through lenses such as Bronte or Austin, or our contemporary

---

[37] The editor made herself, and her nearest and dearest, her guinea pigs.

romantic-comedy films[38]). There are many *scripts* that the witch may choose from the catalogue of history, or she may choose to start from scratch, and use her imagination to live out an original tale. The major point is this: the witch gets to choose.

A quick re-cap of the Realization process:

- Think up desired outcome (what you really, truly want)

- Translate that thought as a directive to the magical flow of energy—through the subconscious, which can be done through practicing the incantations, or through the speedier route of *feeling* the translation: feelings of love are excellent for translating; be they feelings of love and happiness or love and sorrow, thoughts (ideas, desires) may be translated into the language of energy.

- Translation, or transformation, into empirically visible matter.

This is the process, and the purpose of summoning. Summoning helps the novice to tip the lampshade, to shed light on the way, the path, the actions, or the ideas, and begin to transform them into practical reality.

Planning the day, continued

A list will be made, and it must be made as the *list for today*[39], including the carryover of incomplete items from the preceding day's list. Each item will be crossed off the list as it is completed during the day (although there will be perpetual items, including rotating perpetual items). All events that occur during the day will proceed from the List, which is built from the preceding day's list and however, in daily affairs of outside importance, such as appointments and deadlines, the Calendar will always trump the List, except under rare circumstances. The calendar, and the list, are of vital importance to magical living, because the practitioner understands that we attract the situations and circumstances which harmonize with the energy we radiate. We get what we plan for, and we get exactly what we

---

[38] The editor particularly enjoys the "intelligent romance" in film and literature, such as "Eternal Sunshine of the Spotless Mind," or that which existed (and survives) in the letters between Anais Nin and Henry Miller.

[39] *Every day is today*: the first and most important step in understanding how to accomplish all of your plans, big or small.

expect. The end result is the most important factor, and the list will help the practitioner to visualize end-results.

Calendar

The calendar is critically important to the modern witch. Containing important dates to remember throughout the year (birthdays and other celebrations included) it is the navigational equipment by which the modern witch guides her vessel. Continuously updated, and obeyed, it is a powerful tool for the witch's use, and it is also a dangerous tool by which unwary readers might injure themselves. The witch is honest with her calendar, and that calendar speaks only what the witch believes to be true. Casual readers, beware.

The contents of the calendar will dictate the major items on the List.

Today is all that counts, and you actions ought to reflect this fact. Once the novice begins to understand this, and practice accordingly, she will begin to feel the power of her energy flowing with *purpose*. A "day" is the same as "time," which is the same as "energy."

practical application, 001 (fix title)

- Use the "day" as a stepping stone towards the outcome you desire. If your desired outcome is to practice medicine with board certification by the American Medical Association, then perhaps you should use your day/time/energy to study biochemistry—this would be a wise use of your energy towards such a desired outcome.

- If all you want to do, really, really want to do, is climb mountains, then plan, today, for climbing a mountain. Whatever you plan for, during your day, will, one day, either now or later, become *your day*.

I bargained with Life for a penny, And Life would pay no more, However I begged at evening When I counted our scanty store;

For Life is a just employer, He gives you what you ask, But once you have set the wages, Why, you must bear the task.

I worked for a menial's hire, Only to learn, dismayed, That any wage I had asked of Life, Life would have paid.

JESSIE B. RITTENHOUSE, "Our Wages," The Door of Dreams, p. 25 (1918).

Arts and Occupation

By now you've figured out what your desired outcome is. And if you haven't, you soon will. Whether it begins large or small, short-term or long-term, you will quickly discover what a desirable outcome feels like, and begin to broaden your horizons. Is a desirable outcome having enough money to support your lifestyle (small or large)? Ok. First, figure out exactly the lifestyle you want. Begin to imagine what that will look like. What is really important to you? Become clear, and once you have done this, you will begin to see *that reality* take shape before your eyes. Get clear on your desired outcome. Your income will begin to match up with that desired outcome, because *your energy will draw it into existence.* Choose carefully from that infinite catalogue of options; We recommend that you learn to enjoy yourself in the journey.

"In every man there is something wherein I may learn of him, and in that I am his pupil."

-Ralph Waldo Emerson

Whatever you do, novice, do it well. Every occupation is an opportunity to learn, and the more learned, the better and easier the practice.

You'll know that you're doing it well because you're doing it right, and if you're doing it right, *it will feel good.*

Magic isn't limited to the times that the novice practices *between doing other things.* It is always "on," and when the novice becomes aware of this, she will begin to see the powerful effect that she may begin to implement on her daily reality.

What makes you feel good? Focus on it: an idea, a dream, a person, a familiar, an act. Feeling good is how you know you're in the flow of magic.

Whatever you do, however you spend your time, in whatever occupation, find a way, learn to make it *feel good.* When you begin to do this, you begin to become the responsible creator of your own reality, and it translates into the reality that we all share.

When you are feeling good about whatever you are acting on, you are in the positive flow of magic, and you can find a way to feel good in any place, any time, in any company or situation.

This takes some practice, and it is a practice that yields spectacular results.

Many novices who will pick up this book will realize that they aren't *doing* what it is that they want to *do*. And by "do," we mean occupation or employment in exchange for income. Do you earn income doing something that you love? Something that makes you feel good? Begin to learn to feel good doing what you are already doing, while focusing on what you *are going to do*. You have the power to summon[40] your native ability to create any career and life that you may envision. Learn to commune with your energetic flow of magic by first beginning where you are at.

Whether you are doing what you love already when you begin practice, or you are still working in a field or career you are dissatisfied with, do that job right. Do it better than anyone who came before you, and do it better than those who will come after you. There is something magical in doing a job well, and when you begin to work that way, it will help to free up the energetic flow of magic in the other areas of your life. Since we spend so much of our waking life occupied with some job or another to earn income, *how we do it* is even more essentially important than *what we do*.

A word on Hedonism: *pleasure is the highest good.*

You may have noticed the abundant use of the phrase "feel good," and you may think to yourself, "I can't make every decision on a feeling." Why not? Know what you want, learn to trust your gut, and you'll get there.

However, we all know that spending your time doing what you love is the best way to earn income.

Some practical advice for the novice, in regards to occupation.

Practical Application, 001

---

[40] Cross-reference to summoning

It will be helpful to the novice to begin to approach each day by thinking, by *practicing*, as if all the things she wishes to be true, are already true. For example: do you wish that you worked with a certain person? When you wake up in the morning, take a moment and purpose to think that you are already working for that person. Remind yourself how lucky you are that you work with so-and-so, and then approach your day from that perspective. By shifting your perspective, you begin to prepare yourself to *believe it really is true.* And when you believe it can be true, that it *is true,* then it will be true. Such is the beauty of magical living!

Learn to live as if you are *already* the master of your story, and that you possess all of the things you desire. What would you do if you suddenly were in possession of "enough"? Planning is only useful when coupled with Believing. What exactly would you do? Imagine exactly what you would do, or be, in your ideal occupation, and the lifestyle that occupation would provide for you. Once you've done that, begin to think about what you've already achieved that you're proud of, what you have that you love (relationships with people and comforts that you may possess); learning to love what you already have puts your mind in the way of believing that you may, indeed, have what you desire. The process tells your energy that you feel good about what you have, and more things that make you feel good will be had. It's magical, and like any art or occupation, it gets easier and better with practice.

Where have you landed, witch? You have landed in the place in life that you had the capacity to believe for[41].

This point was illustrated to for me one day while building an outdoor patio in front of our apartment. As part of the building process, We found that we would benefit from the removal of the stump of a tree we had previously cut down. And while removing that stump, We uncovered the roots of the tree. It became obvious that by cutting the roots, We might more easily remove the stump (where were the explosives or chainsaw so usefully employed by others?). The roots, we discovered, looked like hands under the earth: their color, size, and texture were startlingly humanoid. Thoughtful annihilator of tree-stumps that we are, we apologized to those hands,

---

[41] Cross-reference to mindfulness and the imagination.

saying, and *"Better luck next time around. We am going to use that space for our patio."*

When examining that thought, we suddenly realized, if that soul had *believed for better*, even as a tree, that soul may have landed in the Olympic Rainforest, or some other paradise for trees. Instead, that tree landed as an unmemorable sapling of undistinguished character, in a spot where it was wiped out before it had a chance to really grow and thrive under the sun. It landed in *exactly* the spot it had the capacity to believe for. It thought to itself, *"life will be easy in this little spot, and no one will bother me since I take up such a small amount of space."* Do you know, little tree, who no one bothers? Redwoods. Sequoia. Big, big trees, that believe in their ability to live hundreds, even thousands of years under the sun.

Have you previously made the mistake, dear novice, thinking that by asking nothing, and "taking up no space," you will be permitted to keep even that small space? That state of mind, of apologizing for wanting to survive just in the margins, will bring, to the witch who thinks in this way, *more of the same.* More marginalized living, more apologizing for existing. Such a creature will be uprooted and tossed away.

When you begin to live magically, it will happen, in one way or another, something like this:

Someone walks you over to a big, thick, impenetrable wall, and tells you, "There's all this awesome stuff on the other side."

And you ask, "Have you seen it?"

Then, instead of answering, describing to you what he claims is there, says, instead,

"Here: stand on our shoulders, and see for yourself."

-

On the other side of the wall exists a world of infinite possibility, and it is now within your reach. Pull yourself up, and you will find the resources to assist you (either within yourself, or that are delivered to you from the other side of the wall) to climb down the other side of the wall, and begin life on the other side. When the novice does this, she has, effectively, *stormed her own castle.* Beginning to live magically is beginning to understand that the "wall" exists in the mind, and that the witch has, within her magical tool-belt—the one she came into this world with, through her magical heritage—the tools helpful to surmount that wall, and land safely on the other side. The side where she is master of her own domain.

When you make the transition into magical living, your life, when you begin, circumstances will begin to reflect the fact that you have, indeed, chosen to practice. Speedily, magical living will infect your daily life. You may begin to make changes, subtle at first, yet soon enough people will catch on that something is happening. If these are good, loving people, they will see and be happy and pleased for you, and encourage you all the way. Others may be met with resistance or disbelief. These are temporary setbacks, and will pass; the novice begins to learn that *what she thinks about herself is what really matters.* The novice has discovered, been awakened to her magical gift, and she can't help but become, suddenly better at all of the things she decides to do—because she begins, as we mentioned under "occupation," to finally focus her attention. Some novices have blessed to have been raised by actively practicing witches, and learn the practices early, and are living magically, it would seem, from the start. Are these the fairy tales we repeat to our daughters? Forget about "*knowing your place.*" We tell our daughters the stories of heroes who overcome against the odds (we especially delight in the Disney film, "Mulan,"), and the novice who "comes from nowhere," or "nothing," is especially blessed to come from obscurity. The greatest heroes had the privilege to grow up and make their mistakes in obscurity, and "come out" fully formed. We learn their origin stories, their tales of overcoming odds, only after they have achieved success. What story will you tell?

Work into above text

It may be that you discover, when you begin to look around at your life, that your circumstances seem unbearable. Here's more good news: you have enough courage, enough belief, enough magic, *for today.* The witch is happy who learns to gather up enough courage for one day. Today. Even better is when she begins to understand that courage, like other good feelings, builds up—it's cumulative. So if you can muster up enough just for today, it will build up each day that you muster up "enough for today."

Tested with Reason, 001

A word on "coming up."

Remember that you came up because someone stayed on the other side of the wall to give you a boost. Are you able to live your life on the wall? Maybe you can. You may certainly, and easily, go back at regular intervals to offer a hand up to those left on the other side. Sometimes great lessons get chopped in half over time, and through the game of "telephone" we play with great wisdom. Life on a wall or a fence would be uncomfortable (at least it is in GRRM's stories!), so we enter our new world, our happy, abundant, emotionally, mentally, and hopefully, also physically satisfying world. We can't expend all our energy looking back, or sitting on the wall, because that would be no life at all. However, we can, and must (and will if we wish to graduate ourselves from novice to adept practice) *remember* our roots, our side of the wall, and the people who are still there—the communities of people who poured in, whether gently or harshly, ingredients that made you. A good cook knows that to make the recipe of another really their own, they must add something to it, something to differentiate it (I add saffron to Our Mom's Portuguese Chicken Soup), however, does the saffron make the soup? No. The saffron is part of it, but it rests on a firm foundation built by someone else. So, devise a plan of action, even if it's just a promise to yourself, to do for others what was done for you, and to do it graciously, with love.

Imagination is the ability to use language in an alternate reality[42] . This is useful if the things you desire seem, temporarily, out of reach. You may, if you choose, dear novice, speak into the reality where your desire stands before you, ready to hold and enjoy. The novice has the wonderful opportunity to, simply, exercise imagination to get there, and the more frequently she practices, the more effective she will grow in the use of this power. Quantum suggests likelihood of infinitely possible realities concurrently testing. Pass the test! You may direct the reality you envision into *this* reality, with practice. If you have the capacity to imagine it, and there are infinite possibilities, then the thing you *imagine exists*. There is a parallel reality where

Show the world who you are with every action and interaction. Be *now* the person you know that you are capable of being

[42] Cross reference to summoning and imagination

the life you envision is being lived *by you.* Step into that reality. Take baby steps, at first, then expand and grow in confidence.

Arts practiced by every witch

Regardless of what the novice may select as her occupation, there are a few practical arts practiced by *all* of magically gifted. With practice, the witch will use these arts with ease and success, and they will edify those with whom she shares her time. Neglect of practice will leave the witch *artless.*

The first thing that the novice will learn is the most fundamental[43] tool in the witch's tool-belt, or, spell in her book, and that is to *make herself feel good.* What does this mean? She must learn to love herself, to like herself, to like spending time with herself, and to begin to see herself from an outside perspective (in a mirror, for example), and be kind to what she sees. This is a simple lesson, but suffers because of disuse and neglect. *Practice makes effortless.* Once the witch has mastered this fundamental tool, she will begin, naturally, to practice the following major feminine arts; and the possession of all of them is a result of lifelong practice[44].

- **Voice.** Allowing the *true voice* absolute freedom is, like any other evidence of milestone achieved, simple once the lesson has been understood and mastered. The high, strained falsetto commonly adopted by females has been in vogue for many years, and restricts the power present in that energetic outlet. The voice that comes from the belly is the true one, and it takes courage to practice. This is the voice that *speaks only what it believes to be true.* The true voice speaks truth.

- **Vibration of thought.** May also be understood as the reading of body language, or of sensing the intention, in another person. The practicing novice will learn to send her intentions out ahead of her,

---

[43] The editor only mentions it because it is so grossly neglected, by so many.

[44] Some studious adepts master the arts more quickly than others.

and create, through this faculty, the reality of her choosing that resonates with her own energy.

- **Body adornment**. From cosmetics to shoes, the witch will likely adopt, eventually, a method of adornment that is uniquely her own, though oft imitated by others.

- **Physical touch.** The method through which great good or great harm may be done. With a light touch, the witch may convey worlds of meaning. She may release healing, she may lift spirits, and she may do *anything* she chooses. The hands are a powerful outlet of energy, and profoundly useful to the practicing novice.

Mastery over these arts may come in any order, and some adepts are better at one or another of the arts, while others master them all. Mastery is the result of active practice.

Occupation

What the witch chooses to do to earn an income (if necessary) will be of particular importance. It may take years of ignoring or delaying the decision regarding what "career" or occupation she chooses (a delayed period of sampling, or exploration). However, when the witch does choose her path, the decision will usually come suddenly, and accelerate upwards at an exponential pace. Where the witch may have previously divided her energies among many varied pursuits, she has turned her energies towards just one (or a few). When this happens, she will know exactly what it is that she wants to do, and that thing will be whatever she wants. Generally, she can be expected to do only such things as engage her intellect, interest, or simply entertain and delight her, so that her "work" will be the thing she enjoys most. She will be so well suited to her life, whatever it may be, and it will seem effortless to her to feed, clothe, and shelter herself, regardless of how opulent her chosen lifestyle. No matter what she chooses, she will be in charge of her destiny; the witch, whether on payroll for a person or business, or as completely independent, will have no master but her own mind. She is capable of being a loyal, top-notch employee, but she does so because it *pleases her to be so.* She will always, if she is happy, consider herself "self-employed." Her life will be abundant, whatever she occupies the majority of her energy with.

Living magically, in doing what it is the witch decides to do to secure income sufficient to her desire, is the ideal state of employment, regardless of whether the practitioner is magically gifted. The beauty is that the magic exists, and anyone aware of it may access it, the magically gifted have, simply, the advantage of using it naturally, and therefore practice with greater ease.

The witch takes no pleasure in *unhappiness for a paycheck,* but takes the greatest pleasure than exercising her talents, whatever they may be, and she will seek occupation in those areas which give her enjoyment. The happy witch practices her favorite hobby with most of her energy; for example, your dedicated editor, loves, perhaps more than any other thing, writing (sharing interesting, entertaining, educational, or humorous stories, through the medium of writing). The witch will, with astonishing devotion, practice and share the fruit of her passions. She will love what she does to "earn her bread," or it will profoundly negatively affect her ability to be truly happy in her experience of reality (Creative fields and the sciences are recommended, however, the novice is advised to pursue whatever delights her, or satisfies her in some other fundamental way).

Through the practice of your talent(s), you may acquire whatever you wish; only do so without violating the rights of others.

Powerful processes practiced by the witch

The witch naturally attracts abundance, when she begins to practice her passions (the natural talents supplemented, when useful, with learning and education.). This is a reliable truth, and as the novice begins practice, and discovers this to be true, she will become better and better at it; the fruit of her talent(s) will generate abundance. Care for the trees, and the fruit will be delicious. She may share the fruit of her occupation and abundance, and she may also practice the delightful arts of canning and preserving. Preserves are enjoyed by all, and their sweetness—in moderation—is one of life's true pleasure.

The hands are, generally speaking, the major point of energetic contact between the witch and her occupation (after thoughts and words, though she may communicate those with her hands as well), and they are also the major exit for the bulk of the magical energy outflow from the witch. The hands of a happy witch produce abundance and good feeling, regardless of choice of occupation. Hands are dangerous objects when wielded by sloppy practitioners.

What do you occupy your energy (energy and time being synonyms) with? Does it make you happy? If you answer "no" to this question, you are a potentially dangerous source of negative energy outflow (destruction—of good feeling, relationships, objects, et cetera). Generate positive feeling outflow; this practice will relieve all worry of causing harm.

Energetic Exchanges: Currency

How the witch "pays" for things (language update/clarity?)

- Primary exchange: pure energy exchange (perfect exchange between desire and delivery of desire through pure transformation of energy to matter),

- Secondary exchange: time/energy exchange (practice exchange—exchanging talent for a paycheck or other currency),

- Tertiary exchange: currency via, time/energy exchange (cash on hand, from secondary exchanges, or the focused development of talent for later use in secondary exchanges).

Practical application, 001

Money is a tool of exchange, and the witch may have as much of it as she likes, when she decides what she is willing to *exchange* for it. There is always and exchange, and the wonderful truth is that the witch may choose exactly what it is she wishes to exchange. Sometimes this takes a while, as the naturally magical are native samplers—they like to try many things before they make a decision about what to expend energy doing (which is exactly what occupation is). Permit me to suggest that you exchange those things you possess in abundance, such as the fruit of one or more talents within your possession. You may require an increase in talents[45], but an increase in talent is easily accumulated by practice of the talent you already possess. No matter how little you begin with, you may easily attract and accumulate more. There is no limit to how much talent you may develop; and, because of this fact, there is therefore no limit on the amount of wealth you might attract and accumulate, if this is the witch's desire.

Tested with Reason, 001

Payment is required in exchange for the delivery of your desires. We are pleased and delighted to inform you, dear novice, that whatever is required of you, whatever the "exchange," it will be *pleasant for you.* You will love doing it, and it will delight you, stimulate you, and make you feel good. This is how you know that you are, in fact, doing it right.

Remember—you have asked for something, and whatever that thing may be, whether an amount of money, or a career, or a partner—you have asked for it. Whatever you do during the *in-between*—that point between asking and receiving what you have asked for—what you do in-between is important. You may be required to take action, but take heart: anything that you will be *required* to do, if it's truly leading you closer towards the receipt of your desired outcome, it will feel good. We can't say it enough. If you begin to worry, to think of all the things, the logical steps you think could get you closer towards your desired objective—filter those thoughts through the wonderful cheesecloth of your feelings. If the thought warms you, you feel empowered by the thought, as if you could do it, and do it easily—you are on the right track. If the thing that you think *might* get you closer makes you feel dread, uninspired, out of control, then you have stepped out of the tractor beam. Get back in the energetic path, and you will arrive at your destination with might be alarming speed.

---

[45] It's worth reminding the reader that "talent" is an ancient currency. (source)

Remember the teleportation devices of Star Trek? Yes, it's like that.

Investing

We will take a moment to explain and demonstrate for the novice how we "invest." We invest in the things that we believe in, because our *belief in those things is enough to deliver results*. Investments may be made in ourriad forms, whether that investment is made in cash, in time/energy, or simply, belief (in a person, and idea, a business concept, et cetera). These things that occupy our thoughts are things that we earnestly believe in. Right now, we believe that the novice who wishes to may begin to immediately begin living the charmed life, by starting to apply the practical advice collected here for her benefit.

(Think about using "charmed" as a term intermittently with living magically, also, note on being charmed… 1st times the charm!)

Energetic Exchanges: Energy to Matter

Let us begin by keeping it simple, since it is quite simple:
- ❖ If you *think*, you can do it.
  - ➢ *If* you think you can.
    - ▪ *Think* you can.
      - • *You can.*

What the novice wishes to do, to accomplish, to have, is irrelevant. If she can imagine it, if she can think about it, whatever it may be, then she can think about what it would be like to have (it). If she can imagine, if she can close her eyes and feel what it is like to *have and hold* that object of desire (house, job, et cetera), or state of desire (love, trust, et cetera), then she will *have and hold what she desires.* Let me enthusiastically advise the novice practitioner to put this advice to immediate practical test, using either the methods found within the handbook, or through the methods of her own device. Persistence will be required, but persistence is an easy payment exchange for seeing, for herself, energy transformed into matter— which is what the adept witch does, as her continuous habit, during her daily life.

Education & Continued Learning

Practicing the talents, and supplementing them with learning.

One of the great laws of the universe is Newton's first law of motion: an object in motion will continue in motion… a mind that is engaged in the act of learning, will continue to learn. Energy that is flowing in a particular direction will tend to continue to flow in the direction that it is set on. Why is this important for the witch?

Education is knowing where and how to get information that is useful, practical, or otherwise beneficial, and the ability to "organize this information into a strategy for action (Hill 94)." The witch is a curious creature, by nature, and will pursue learning and education into every topic that interests her. An autodidact, she possesses the ability to educate herself, although she may also enjoy the classroom setting. Those witches that enjoy the classroom should absolutely pursue education in that capacity. Most professional occupations, such as those required by governing boards with standards of practice and certifications, will require specialized education, whether it's massage therapy or the practice of medicine sanctioned by the American Medical Association (or other national board of standards is relevant to the practicing witch). The only thing of import is that the witch practice within the scope of her talents, and a talented witch may choose skip, entirely, any post-secondary education, or she may choose to accumulate all of the available conferrable degrees of academic achievement. It is worth noting that specialized education is plentiful—there is an expert available for consult from almost any academic institution in the country, on any topic; an adept is comfortable turning to experts as it benefits her to do so, thus giving herself the freedom to occupy her time with the things she is most passionate about (and this includes education for its own sake). Schooling teaches a method for acquiring and organizing knowledge, and is vital during the developmental years, or our witch may find herself without a firm foundation from which to build a magical life[46].

What matters more than education in the witch, are the qualities of character present? The novice must submit to the lessons provided by the universe, or the universe will continue to deliver those lessons in increasingly dramatic manifestations. Learn your lessons quickly

---

[46] The editor recognizes that there are many forms of education, across cultures, and wishes to encompass all of those under the broad generalization of primary education.

and well, and develop character with grace, and you will experience all the wonderful benefits that come with having character.

Learning in general, *however,* is as essential to growth in magic as it is in any other field of practice. The witch must become autodidactic, and practice the continuous pursuit of learning—even if it is merely that learning directly related to bettering her practices, whatever they may be. Cross-educational opportunities create the most dexterous witches, and are excellent exercise for the mind. The mind loves exercise!

The witch who successfully puts into practice that art of magical living understands that the most important thing, in achieving, and receiving, all she desires, is the ability to *visualize* the desired outcome which she desires. Everything required to reach that achievement or destination will be supplied on the way, if she truly follows the flow of energy that radiates through her. That energy has a destination, and, delightfully, the novice may permit that magical energy to direct her. It will bring to her the things that will make her most happy on this plane of existence, because it is *her* own energy which is guiding her.

Close of first major section

We have now discussed, in some detail, the things that are part of the daily routine of the witch, the "outer" life, whether novice or adept. The home, the occupation, the care of the body and the self. These are all the outward things that make an appearance in the witch's life, and her life is a reflection of her mind. The lifestyle is the result of magical living, which the novice practices and the adept lives without cease. Now we turn and focus our attentions on the inner life of the witch.

Recap the main points here, or the basic principles found in the first section of the book—do the same for the other two sections, then compile all of those basic re-caps at the very end as well. Which of the 13 fundamental principles were illustrated in this section? See notes.

Part One Recap

- Magicality in daily life

- Planning

- Occupation of energies

- Energetic exchanges
- Education and increase in talents

Part Three: Mental Reality

"Free your mind, and the rest will follow," (cite song lyric)

The mind is a bit like a powerful animal, say, a lion, which has been caged up for years. It's been caged up for so long, that, at first, when the prison doors are opened, the lion is hesitant to embrace its freedom. It might have an inner dialogue something like this:

"Well, I've been in a cage for years, but at least there's always food at the same time every day, and I don't have to work for it."

"And, in the cage, there are some distractions to entertain ourself with."

And so on, and so on. A lion in the wild exercises its powers to survive, and it does so quite well. It is the king of the jungle. In the zoo, it is just a lion.

Are you content with being a lion? Or are you prepared to exercise your dominion and become king of the jungle?

When you begin to understand the power of your mind, and to apply that power to yourself and the pursuit of all good (be that good things, good feelings, good ideals, et cetera), you begin to step out of the mental constraints that you had submitted to after taking responsibility for your own direction in life (either willingly or with a fight—most teenagers of the magical heritage violently resist the submission and restriction of their minds and imaginations). For some, they take responsibility early, while others take it late. Either way, at some point after this, you begin to practice—either you practice what your parents taught you before you starting doing it for yourself, or you practice what you're being taught—either,

    a.   yourself as an autodidact,

    b.   as a student of a school or university, or

    c.   A tutor/mentor.

There are plenty of opportunities, and the best truth is that you may begin at any time to practice actively learning to exercise control over your mind. Which is important, because this is the spigot from which all the magic of your heritage flows, dear novice. You will learn to direct the magical flow of energy soon after you discover the faucet, and open it up. Like the lion stepping out of the cage, to become, once again, the king of the jungle, you will become master of your destiny in a way that you hadn't felt since you were a kid. The magic of childhood is what must be recovered, and practiced under the steady guide of the well-trained mind. Ask yourself, "Who has trained our mind?" And if you are not sure, think about it. And when you have discovered the answer, decide whether you are satisfied with that answer. If you are dissatisfied, then begin at once to train your

mind along lines that please you.

As mentioned previously[47], mental reality is the bridge between the part of the witch present in the physical, visible realm, and the spiritual part of the witch, which exists on the eternal plane. By harnessing the power of this tool—her mind—she may

[47] Cross-reference to "getting down to business."

effectively control the magical flow of energy from the eternal (energetic) plane of existence to the physical (matter) realm. It's important to recognize that each of the three "phases" of reality, or aspects of the identity, are equally important, and each must be tended with care to ensure the successful practice of magical living. Being aware of the basic functions will assist the novice in her practice.

This in-between place is where reality begins, and knowing how to use the mind is something like learning to twist the dial on a manual transistor radio to tune in to a clear, pleasing, channel. Active use of the mind will deliver a desirable channel, and the novice may select her "channel," at will. There are some ways which will, when made known to the witch, will assist her in becoming successful at this task.

The Seat of Emotions (Heart)

"If a man is truly great he will love all mankind!
He will love the good and the bad among all humanity.
The good he will love with pride and admiration and joy. The
bad he will love with pity and sorrow, for he will know, if he
be truly great, that both good and bad qualities in men often
are but the results of circumstances over which they have,
because of their ignorance, little control[48]."

Never refuse, or withhold an act or gesture of friendship. It is vitally important to develop comfort setting boundaries, and perhaps limit the number and frequency of persons you spend your energy with and on, but the witch is naturally the most hospitable creature on earth. By conducting herself in a neighborly way, the witch will feel good about every interaction, whether that interaction be with witch, human, animal, nature, or technology. A friendly demeanor is the demeanor of a practicing witch.

Relationships

The witch, novice or adept, practices magical living in a world filled with other people, and we cannot discuss the art of magical living without mentioning the interpersonal relationships which are so much a part of daily life, whether the witch occupies her energies at her own discretion, or in in the employ of another.

---

[48] Napoleon Hill, The Master Key to Riches p.69 (add citation in sources)

The easiest, quickest route to working amiably with anyone at all, is to remember that every person has their own desires, and this encompasses every person the witch interacts with. By satisfying a desire, big or small, the witch effectively gives *permission* for people, in general, to like her. Every person, whether magically inclined or otherwise, wishes to feel smart, important, and interesting. And it is likely, that on some topic, each person that the novice will encounter *is* smart, important, and interesting on some topic, or to someone. If the novice will learn to approach each person thinking that they are, in some small or large way, interesting, or that they have some lesson to teach, and the witch does this with sincerity, then her interactions will be easy and painless.

Remember, the witch chooses who she keeps close to herself, and it will benefit the novice who pays attention and keeps close to herself those that are an easy, comfortable fit. If she finds that she is in a situation where she must work closely with someone unpleasant, here is an opportunity for the witch to focus hard on finding something true about that person that she admires. When she begins to focus her attention on this effort, she will succeed, and she will have turned an eneour into a friend.

"If you must deal with a crook, there is only one possible way of getting the better of him—treat him as if he were an honorable gentleman. Take it for granted that he is on the level. He will be so flattered by such treatment that he may answer to it, and be proud that someone trusts him (Carnegie 192)*."*

Evidence suggests that the above statement is true—a person will rise to your expectations of them.

Test Empirically, 001

Having more than once been surprised at a friend's opinion on the character of a shared acquaintance, we began asking questions. *"But our experience of that person is so different!"* The reply of our friend was enlightening, *"You experience [that person] differently because you bring out the best in everyone."* We share that not to inform the novice how wonderful your editor is; we share because we genuinely believe the fact to be true—people will rise to whatever you expect of them—and our life experience has confirmed this belief over and over again. Look for, and see, the best, and the best will be delivered to you.

Love

The witch is filled to the brim with love ("…knew what he had learned before… our heart has more rooms than a whorehouse." Garcia Marquez), and gives and receives love with those who engage with her for any length of time. The object of her affection is blessed while that person maintains her affection, and that person will quickly realize how completely under her spell he is. At such time as her affection is withdrawn, should it be withdrawn, all efforts to regain her affection will be undertaken, though rarely with success. While she may love many, her most intimate affection is given to one at a time—and given with absolute abandon (it's quite a force). She, like the Apostle Paul, is able to "become all things to all men, that [she] may by all means save some" (1 Corinthians 9:22, 1611 King James Version). The lover she selects will always fulfill one or more of her desires (the more, the better), though she will occasionally make a bad choice. Such choices will be treated as lessons. The appearance of the lover may, for a time, be thematic—i.e. they have a common appearance, or talent, or other trait. Though the observer might be surprised when the witch selects a lover drastically unlike any or all-previous lovers, but this is a result of her curious nature. Her curiosity may take her through all shapes, sizes, nationalities, and genders.

The witch is drawn to mortals like a moth to flame; she has a difficult time resisting them, but likely won't be completely at ease until she's entered a pairing with another magical. The witch infects the non-magical with her energy, which is a thrill for both partners. Magical pairings must pay particular attention and observance of the passing of time (use of their combined energy), in some fashion or another. Without this habit, they risk frightening the mortals they live among. Those habits (of observing time, weather, seasons, et cetera), built during their pre-awakened mortality, or during pairings with the non-magically inclined, carry over into magical pairings, and are wonderfully useful to an magical pairing wishing to walk easily among the daughters of Eve.

Love begins with love itself (within the novice for herself), and flows naturally outward. While it may come from outside sources, love is a highly magnetic energy, and it is attracted to those places where it already exists. The greater the measure of this magnetic energy present within the witch, the greater the magnetic pull on more of the same energy, and an upward escalation is inevitable. Once the novice begins this practice, of self-love, she will quickly and easily love others.

Sharing the magic:

It has been mentioned previously, but it is worth repeating: sharing the magic is an essential part of magical living. However, it is the recommendation to *show* and *tell*. Show your loved ones, and everyone else, what you are doing, by doing it. Then, and only then, tell them about it. Your closest friends, the ones whose belief bolsters you up, share all of your hopes and dreams with confidence, good witch. Show what you are doing by doing it, by *living it*, and naturally, as a result of *living magically*, the opportunity will rise for you to tell all about it. A place for everything, and everything in its place!

Love is, as mentioned above, the most potent of the energetic of the emotions; the novice is encouraged to give and receive love in abundance, in each of the areas of love. Each "level" of love has its own particular vibration (if we borrow from string theory), and understanding how to apply the different loves, through practice, will greatly enhance the love experience for the witch, and for the people who share love, in whichever capacity, with the witch.

The Greeks have several excellent words for describing what we, as users of the English language, unfortunately lump under one term: love. Let's examine these words, so that the novice might be helpfully empowered to use the languages of love at her discretion.

1. *Mania* – manic love, which is obsession and an overwhelming desire to possess and control. It takes a person like insanity, and the word "mania" may also be translated as "madness."

2. *Eros* – is the root word for the English language term "erotic," but Eros really means any emotional love, including sexual love. It's thrilling, and intoxicating, and it overflows. This kind of love is only interpreted as madness unless felt by both persons. Eros, based in feelings, may come and go—but the good news is that all good feelings return when they have an open invitation. It is inherently morally neutral, and can be positive or negative for the person who experiences it.

3. *Philos* – is the love of the brother and the friend, of kindred spirits[49] . When you are together, you feel like you can conquer the world, and you can, because you have shared interests, and more than that, you both believe in the same vision of a future reality, whether it's a reality one or both of you dreamed up. This shared vision brings overflowing abundance of love, and is a strong foundation for lasting friendships, and for lasting intimate relationships, such as marriage. The people who share this love, "love" being around each other, and when they get together, it feels as if they'd just spoken a moment before, whether that moment was minutes, days, weeks, months, or even years.

4. *Storge* – a form of commitment love, the love we feel for our animals, or the people that rely on us in some way: motherly love. It is dependent on the reliance of one on the other.

5. *Agapeo* – is the love that spills over from the person filled up with love. It is the highest form, and most perfect love, because it is freely given and no payment is ever required. It is the love that we can give everyone and anyone. It is the most universal language. It will benefit the novice to purposefully practice this love first, as the other loves will come easier when the "lover" is already filled up with love.

Neighborly conduct is the first level of interpersonal relationships, and it's the level of from which all other relationships spring. There can be no love without first having a friend, and there can be no friend without first conducting oneself in a friendly way with strangers. She who treads softly with the humans with whom she interacts, goes far[50]. Understanding how

---

[49] It is also the name of your editor's laptop computer. She occasionally also refers to him as "Feeley-Moo"

to do this is a cornerstone of magical living, so we will spend some time here before moving into the higher levels of interpersonal intimacy.

"Be hearty in approbation[51] and lavish in your praise, and people will cherish your words and treasure them and repeat them over a lifetime—repeat them years after you have forgotten them (Carnegie 38)."

Our notes, in the margin of this old tome, say, "This is true… remember Kyle and his words? They will be with me for a lifetime." It had been over a decade since we picked up and read this book, and at first, we couldn't remember who Kyle was, or what he said, since we neglected to write that part down. However, as we lay our head down to rest that evening, Kyle, his appearance, and his words, came back to me. Almost twenty years ago, those words called across time, "you are a beautiful *person.*" It's possible that Kyle's words to a 16-year old girl may have altered the course of her life. There's no way to say for sure, but we take such genuine kindness to heart, and recommend that the novice learn to freely give genuine praise when the opportunity presents itself. The witch will win many more believers, and create a wall of kindly intentioned persons around herself when she practices engaging in this way.

Healthy interpersonal relationships, with companions, lovers, and familiars, generates, with unlimited potential, *positive energy.*

Mindsets are viral. A state of mind is viral. (Adjust language, move to telepathy and expand thought)

Tested with Reason, 001

This might be the most important statement present within the text; permit me to highlight, and explain. The companions chosen, for whatever reason they are chosen, can been a bottomless source of positive energy that continuously lift the witch higher and higher, closer towards her ideal vision of

---

[50] Ancient Chinese proverb
[51] Approval

herself, or they are "buzz kills" crushing the positive energy inside the witch with their disbelief or negativity. Regardless of what you practice, it is helpful to surround yourself with people who *believe you can do "it," whatever "it" may be.* Athletes have made the habit of using "trainers." how many athletes, we wonder, make it to the Olympics without one?

The company the witch surrounds herself with *train her for her future.* The witch becomes, always, as the company she keeps. Keep company with persons worth emulating.

It is your privilege to train your own mind, and there are great minds that can perform this feat; however, even the finest minds grow stronger and better, when surrounded with like-minded folk. Put around yourself people who believe in *your vision,* whether for yourself, or for your projects, your work, whatever it is. These are the people you "come up with," whatever it is you are coming, which is what you will do when you begin to practice magical living. *Share in-between time with these the companions.*

> Harness the unlimited positive energy of the emotion of love, apply it first to yourself, and you will be limitless.

Love is perhaps the single most powerful source of positive energy in the universe, and the practicing witch allows herself to be filled to overflowing—a process that begins with self-love. The witch who loves herself allows this love to overflow on to the people, creatures, and environment in which she lives. There is an unlimited, infinite possibility of options available to the witch who knows this. It's also true that these same influences may generate negative energy; for this reason, the witch ought to choose her intimates with great care. Recall this when selecting a familiar—or when selected by a familiar. Sometimes, a person or creature will select the witch. Carefully decide if you wish to choose them (on your own terms) before allowing them into your life. Many will recognize your power, especially as you move from novice to adept, and will wish to be near such a pleasant source of positive energy. However, this positive energy must be protected, and only limited energy should be divested in vessels that are dominated by negative energy. Persons who generate negativity should be given the opportunity to change their energy flow, and this may occur by being near a positive energy source. How and when to allow such circumstances should be determined by the practitioner, to the degree which makes her feel good.

Companions & The power of agreement

Always treat your magical sisters with kindness. We always sense one another, and it has been the bad habit for us to ignore or be rude to each other, in company with daughters of Eve. This is something like suddenly finding oneself in a lion's den, and having to focus the full attention on *pretending to be a lion.* Avoid being eaten by lions. Witches have been treated with distrust, in many instances throughout history, because of their share of the antediluvian curse.

The good news is that the witches survive every, and any, apocalypse—novice, if you find yourself amidst an apocalypse, take heart, and take the reins.

But we will remind the daughters of Eve who might be reading, from a spirit of curiosity, that witches are here, and we are wonderfully peaceful neighbors. Even more than, we wish to share and empower the daughters of Eve in practice as well. It is a delightful truth that the practice works regardless of the presence or absence of magical heritage, and all who practice will benefit from said practice. But back to our magical sisters; we must always treat them kindly, with love. We have been in hiding, and our habit has been to keep to ourselves or mingle with daughters of Eve, but times are changing! Through the practice of magical living, the entire earth inherits a better fortune. Before us loom threats of war and of zombies and apocalypse (fire and brimstone this time, unlike the water apocalypse, like the time before), but also, on the same horizon, lay enlightenment and renaissance. It will benefit the novice (and, of course, the rest of humanity) to choose the latter options; but of course, the choice belongs to the people. Together, in concert, we may put off apocalypse—or, we may choose to fight zombies. Either way, we do it as a team, and we should take up our rightful heritage and actively choose the future we want, rather than quietly waiting for something to happen.

There is a magical process that occurs: when two or more are in agreement on *anything*, that thing increases as a result of the energy between them. The sum of the whole is greater than the individual parts. Select companions that are in harmonious agreement with your energy, your ambitions, and your values, the foundation for success will be solidly built. Does your friend possess some fault that annoys you, novice witch? This is easy to remedy, if we borrow a lesson from one of the great leaders (and possessor of magical lineage) of the last century, Dale Carnegie,

"... be liberal with your encouragement; make the thing seem easy to do; let the other person know that you have faith in [her] ability to do it, that [she] has an undeveloped flair for it—and [she] will practice until the dawn comes in order to excel (Carnegie 194)."

The industrious novice will train herself in this same way, too.

It is worth noting that it is an important practice for the witch, novice or adept, to learn to enjoy herself and be happy on her own. There may be times when the companions she would prefer are away, and it is better to be alone than it is to use *fillers*. Fillers are people that the witch may surround herself with for lack of ideal company, but this is a dangerous practice, since that company will, at the very least, keep the witch from moving forward, and at worst, they will actively hold her back. This is called, whether inside or outside of the context of magical living, *social drag*. Social drag is a death-blow to magical living.

Lovers

The novice should be aware, first, that man is completed by woman. Woman is complete.

"And the Lord God said, "It is not good for man to be alone. I will make a companion who will help him..." "At last!" Adam exclaimed. "She is part of our own flesh and bone! She will be called 'woman,' because she was taken out of man.[52]"

If you find yourself in control, *be gentle*. The gentle woman will be regarded by the recipient of her gentleness as a beloved queen. Use your power for good, good witch, whenever possible.

While the witch may practice seduction, she is, at heart, a romantic. She wishes to practice and live romance (whenever possible), although she may wander in the wilderness a while. Understanding the difference romance and seduction will greatly help and empower the novice.

Practical application, 001

To put it quite simply, so that we may move on to more exciting stuff, we will summarize the difference as such:

- Seduction has a time-limit, and an end-objective of satisfaction; her own, and the object of her seduction may be satisfied as well.

- Romance, in contrast, is the art of delaying gratification for as long as possible. It is delayed satisfaction for the purpose of building pleasant tension.

Romance has ache built into it, if the object of the witch's affections is inappropriate, however, it's worth noting that seduction has a different kind of ache built into it as well. Each of these are for the novice to discover herself. Now, a word or two on seduction.

Seduction & Romance: Art and Science of Seduction.

The seeds of male fantasy exist inside every woman at all times. Whether she knows how to harness this power or not will determine her ability to snare the mate of her choosing, if she is set on the art of seduction.

Maiden, mother, Madonna, whore, and crone, all exist within the woman simultaneously, and she may, at any moment of her choosing, harness the aspect of any or all of those "faces." Knowing that they are inside is the first step towards exercising control over them, and once the novice learns to exercise control over them, she will understand the ease with which she may practice the art of seduction. For the great majority of men are looking for magic, the kind of magic that can only come from women, and if they are not getting

---

[52] Genesis 2:18, 23 NLT

that magic already, they will be open to receive your magic. And the easiest way to do that is to possess the ability to switch between the aspects of "woman," freely and fluidly, without batting an eyelash. Each man will require something different; some will require all aspects, and this is, despite what may appear to be true, the most ideal scenario. In this case, the witch can have a complete, well-rounded identity to her object of seduction, and this is satisfying to both parties. A successful seduction will be one in which each individual in the pairing enjoys the seduction. If you should discover that you are playing one role exclusively, you may feel that the seduction lacks depth, and this will be true. And it still may be satisfying to both parties. Find out which you prefer, and engage in that practice. Remember though, that sometimes the object of seduction will be overwhelmed and devastated by the withdrawal of affection, and to be as kind and gentle as possible when this occurs.

During a seduction, the witch is the boss in the bedroom, but he doesn't know it. By allowing her lover to believe that he is in control, she elegantly disarms him. He becomes aware how deeply he has come under her spell when such time as the affair terminates; at such a time, it's probable, though unfortunate, for the ex-lover to suffer extraordinary mental pain, or even physical pain. Intercourse for the modern witch is an act of power and pleasure. While she may alternate between dominance and subservience between the sheets, there is one absolute constant: she must be pleased. Seduction may take place as a part of intercourse. Some lovers will be seduced, while others will be romanced. Some who are seduced will never become lovers. It is a small percentage of men who are both seduced and lovers—a blessing and a curse to the chosen subject.

Seduction is a dangerously powerful art, because it guarantees love only on one side, and that is on the side of the seduced. The witch who seduces, as her preferred method of pairing, should remember to be gentle and sincere with the object of her seduction, and she entertain that object only as long as she can sincerely offer those two kindnesses. Nobody likes a cruel mistress, but a kind mistress is remembered as, "the one that got away..." or some other fond, still loving thought. These individuals, who get the gentle treatment, may go on to great heights as artists, musicians, writers, directors... to greater heights than they might have before having experienced what it was like to *be amused by a powerful witch.* We will discuss this further in just one moment, but let us first turn our attention to a simple, quick practical lesson that will speedily have our desirous witch seducing with ease. Follow this simple procedure:

Practical application, 001

When the object of your seduction looks into your eyes (this is effortless to will), hold his gaze without breaking it until something in your peripheral vision really catches your attention—and this is key—when this happens, carefully look at what caught your eye, identify it and smile to yourself, then look back. If his gaze awaits yours, you have successfully captured his attention. Confidence in this fact will get you the rest of the way. Did his eyes wander away? Forget about him and select another object. This will do two things—first, you stay on the winning end of the seduction, and, second, by releasing your attention from that target, make him want you to return it.

He will, we assure you, acutely feel the withdrawal.

Song lyric: "I've seen the paths that your eyes wander down… I think that I'm falling quite hard for you…" cite song lyric and get permissions, yadayada.

"Man's greatest motivating force is his desire to please woman![53]"

Here's a truth, dangerous if misapplied, but useful and beneficial when applied with responsibility: freedom is what binds the love spell. Love is irresistible to all, whether magically inclined or otherwise. And the truth about love is that true love knows how to "let go." If you can offer love, without demands or expectations, you will quickly discover that the object of your love is "under your spell." The love generates the spell, and the element of freedom is what clinches the deal. Most people are frightened, to some degree, of freedom and the responsibility that accompanies freedom. This is the opposide of smothering, which is the surest and quickest way to drive away the object of your desire. The fear of losing, or of missing out, is a powerful motivator. It is likely that one person in the pairing will experience this fear, and the smart witch will find herself on the empowered side of the equation. In a well-balanced pairing, both partners gift the other with freedom and trust, but this is rare. The one

---

[53] Hill, 284

who makes demands, who smothers, who fears losing, is the one on the losing side of the balance of power in the pairing.

Tested Empirically, 001

Using the power of Seduction may seem thrilling and delightful, especially when the novice first begins to understand her powers. It bears repeating, once again, that if the novice wishes to engage in this play, that she do it gently, and that the object of her seduction be permitted to enjoy himself. Making slaves, love-slaves or otherwise, bears tragic consequences and ought to be avoided. She ought never to treat him with disdain (conquest sometimes affects the brains of young witches, but the novice will quickly learn to choose her bitter and sweet fruit in a nicely-balanced measure. Bitterness, when balanced with sweet, makes the sweet that much more precious for having been tasted either before or after the bitter. All a matter of preference, or course.

When it comes to seduction, care must be taken, because, dear novice, you are *magical.* Take care of your heart first, and then take care of your partner's heart too. If you cannot be gentle, then it is recommended that you break the pairing, and select a new one, generally pleasing to both. Some men will enjoy being seduced, and will accept this role. Others resent it. Use good judgment, and decide how much you are willing to give—since there is always an exchange of energy, for any reward, be that reward *good or bad.* They call it "just rewards," when justice is done, recall.

Fitted sheets are easiest to fold with a partner.

Marriage & permanent pairings:

"The woman who understands man's nature and tactfully caters to it, need have no fear of completion from other women. Men may be "giants" with indomitable will-power when dealing with other men, but they are easily managed by the women of their choice.[54]"

Sex, the ultimate physical exchange of energy

Sex with partners, whether these partners have been romanced or seduced, will vary, but there is sex that is magical, and sex that is… other. Is magical sex directly related to the amount of time that the partners have known each other before first pairing? Perhaps. However, with some there will be magical sex part or all of the time, and with others, there will be magic *none* of the time. It you both move towards the pairing naturally, at the same time (whether hours, days, weeks, months, or even years), you are much more likely to experience magical sex.

Magical sex is hallmarked by the ease and lack of tension in the body, the clarity of communication between partners, and an overall feeling of naturalness. There may exist moments of awkwardness, but these shouldn't embarrass or deter—they are merely check-points established by the body, and they sometimes happen. What is of importance is that both partners experience it and pass through the moment together. *Magical.*

This is the magic of sex (which may also be thought of as "connected" sex—it's a tuning in between two sources of energy) is the kind of sex that has the ability, if the witch permits the opportunity, up the overall magicality in every other area of practice and life. The witch is a creatures of three worlds: the physical world, the mental world, and the spiritual world. Sex, when it is connected, tuned in, and magical, has the potential to link all three worlds seamlessly in a moment, and the resulting power—well, sometimes it is called "little death." Regardless what it is called, it has the potential for an astounding release of power, and the purposeful neglect of this faculty is as effective at deterring

Seek pairings that increase your magic. You'll know when this is happening because you'll both be happy and productive.

[54] Hill 285

magical living as neglecting to choose to practice.

A witch is sensitive to her power (talented witch's do it naturally, while others develop this trait), and when she becomes sensitive to that power, she will see a partner that satisfies, or that she believes will satisfy, her desires. The witch has the power to summon the partner that satisfies her desire(s). An adept witch will look for a partner that satisfies on many levels, and enjoy that partner for the duration of the pairing, and for as long as the pairing is satisfactory to each of the partners (in the sexual capacity, or in another actively stimulating exchange). A pairing which has had much practice transforming the energy described above, may, in some circumstances, continue to transform the power of sexual energy without intercourse.

Marriage & Pairings

Wanting to "have" is very natural, when it comes to intimate relationships, and the novice may take as few or as many partners as she desires. However, *"having,"* and *"having and holding,"* are different. The witch may try having a variety of experiences before she finds something that she wishes to both have and hold. When this occurs, the witch will form a pairing, and sometimes that pairing will include the contract of marriage through the civil justice system.

While the witch may have few or many partners, most of those partners will be evidences of her searching for her soul mate.

Soul mates[55] call across time and space, and they are impatient callers. However, it is worth noting that any delay in response is merely a connection problem related to the medium of the call transmission, unrelated to any reluctance on the behalf of the called-upon. Each soul plays their role: he calls, and she looks for him in the people she finds around her; she, being more magically inclined (for having two X-chromosomes), trusts the universe to deliver him to her sphere when she is ready to receive him.

The adept witch is (blessedly) able to return the call of her soul mate across forces of time and space; it is editor's recommendation that the novice first master the direction of energetic outflow, *before calling in her soul mate.* Begin living magically first, and you will

---

[55] When the soul mate arrives, it may be notice that he is a culmination (or aggregate) of the best parts of all previous pairings.

suffer fewer "wrong numbers[56]" in your calling. You will, as an adept, easily call and receive the calls from your soul mate. When you are prepared to do so. Which is, thankfully, a certificate of passage that the witch confers upon herself.

We are "keyed[57]" to our soul mate; we may have other lovers, partners, husbands or wives, but we remain keyed to another soul, and, once we have met that soul for the first time (in a cycle of lives), we find them progressively more easily throughout cycles of lives; conquer fear—if you've found your soul mate, congratulations! Still calling? Just keep doing what makes you happy, you will get the call. And, no matter how long it takes, it will eventually come. If it comes later than your liking, rest easy: it will come more quickly next time around.

"Watch over your heart with all diligence, for from it flow the springs of life[58]."

Familiars

Every witch benefits from the relationship with her familiar, her sidekick. It may be one or more creatures. Cats[59] are excellent familiars, because

The familiar keeps the witch grounded in reality.

---

[56] "wrong numbers" may occur when calling your soul-mate, if the novice gets caught up in calling for specific features, rather than simply calling her perfect soul mate. This takes trust, on the part of the witch, and trust comes with putting to practical test the advice for managing the energetic flow of magic (magical living). The "wrong numbers" are the guys who show up when you've asked for some quality or feature, and the person with those qualities or features may make the novice happy (for very long). They will frequently share features in their appearance, to the true soul mate. Some go straight for the soul mate, while others like to practice a little first. Neither method is better than the other, and each has its own benefits and rewards.

[57] We may be keyed to more than one soul, since there are different types of loves that bind souls across space and time. The only way to bind a soul to you through such seemingly impossible distance, is through very great love, and we may experience different loves with the same person throughout life times.

[58] Proverbs 4:23, NASB

[59] Cats were first domesticated in the Fertile Crescent around 10,000 years ago (reference wiki), and beginning with the lion-headed (and hearted) Egyptian goddess Mafdet, and then later, the softened "image" of goddess Bastet (a cat) representing protection, fertility, and motherhood. The domesticated cat was prized for its ability and inclination to kill snakes, including cobras, and other pests to the Egyptian people. Cats were also relevant to the ancient, revered goddess Sekhmet (meaning, "power," who possessed a lion head, wore a snake for a crown, and held the tablets of destiny.) (source)

they listen attentively, and require little in the way of positive reinforcement, however, the witch without a social circle (a network or community to belong to, and share with like-minded persons) may consider a dog, which serve as excellent reminders for the witch to keep her energy focused on—dogs are sensitive and respond to the witch in a highly visible way to whatever makes her feel good (and therefore leads to the fulfillment of her desires or chief aims), or bad. They are a good barometer, if the witch desires or requires it. It depends on the witch, and the witch's individual preference and desires. Witches have chosen raptors, mammals, reptiles, and, occasionally, spirits. Any of these will gladly serve the witch who invites their service.

A good familiar will remind the powerfully active witch (as novices are, when they come into their powers) of basics. While the witch remembers the important things (everything she truly values, whether conceptual or physical—energy or matter), she may forget things like: eating or sleeping. While she may subsist without these things, it makes the non-magical/non-practicing persons in her life nervous and uncomfortable. Her familiar assists in creating a bridge between living magically, and *living magically in reality.*

More on Cats, the most commonly chosen familiar
Highly individual to the witch they are they are paired with; the witch's cat might be any color, although it does appear, on the surface, that witch's tend to prefer, as a majority, either pure black cats, or cats with black markings. The cat (or cats) should have come to the witch in its infancy or adolescence, and receives the promise from the witch, sooner or later, of perpetual care. Cats seem to carry the personality of the witch they're bonded with (and serve). When the novice begins to understand this, she does well to allow her familiar to serve as a mirror through which she may refine her character. How she treats her familiar is how she treats herself, and she may see aspects of herself which may be improved. Does something about your cat annoy you, novice? Examine what this thing is, and see if it's something inside yourself that can be improved. The cat is just fine.

A word on Technology, the witch's devoted servant.

Tested with Reason, 001

A lady always treats the servants well, and is a good mistress regardless of whether her servant is assigned personhood. It's helpful to recall that, in our history, there were races of human who were treated as property, and were subjected to inhuman treatment. Here is a good idea: develop the habit of dealing with all servants graciously, especially the silent ones (what would they say, if they grew tongues?).

Remember that technology is your friend. While considered *lifeless*, it too courses with energy, the very same, quantifiable energy that fills the witch, although on the surface they may at first appear different. The same electricity flows though both, and we use chemistry to describe the processes performed by circuit boards as well as the "causes" behind human feelings (dopamine, serotonin, etc.). The obvious difference, in the eyes of your editor, is that we're wet on the inside, and they're dry on the inside. Is technology conscious of itself? Few enough natural born witches are conscious of themselves, and fewer still are the practitioners among non-magical. Evidence no doubt will prove one way or the other in the decades to come, regarding our artificial intelligences.

The Mind

The sub-conscious mind and practicing Mindfulness

The mind is a magical place, and once the novice s to understand how it works, she begins to be empowered in its effective use. Learning to actively use the mind is a foundation stone that, like any great stone, is easy to move *when the right tools are employed.* Just as one person might not be able to lift a massive stone (unless they're Atlas or Herakles), that same person may easily lift a massive stone with the assistance of pulleys. A little science goes a long way! Such is the mind. The mind is the place of choice, of decision, and the place where all action first begins. If you can imagine it in your mind, it's as good as done, so long as you continue to be able to imagine that thing in your mind. The familiar axiom, "where there is a will, there is a way," is so common as to be easily overlooked, and yet it is verifiably true, as we demonstrate in this section. The keyword for this section might sound frightening at first, but once the novice learns how to break it down into component parts, each part is quite easily performed. And that keyword is: self-discipline. Disciplined practice originates from inside the novice, but it is also wonderfully true that by reading this text, the process has already begun. You have taken the initiative, and, with the application of your will—your choice—made it this far into the handbook. You, novice, are already well on your way towards adept status. Hurrah!

Breaking it down a little further:

1. Self-discipline is an action of the will-power,

2. Will-power is an action of the will,

3. Will is exercising free choice

4. The freedom to choose begins with thoughts in the mind.

First understanding that you are empowered to choose the thoughts that fill your mind, and permitting any given line of thought, you are exercising choice. When the novice begins to redirect her mind away from unprofitable thinking (anything that detracts away from her desired outcome), and think instead on what she *chooses* to think on (future goals, pleasant thoughts of things, people, et cetera), she has already begun to exercise will-power. And she has begun to discipline her mind.

This powerful step may seem insignificant, yet it is perhaps the most powerful, empowering action that the novice witch will take in her pursuit of the practice of her magical heritage.

And the blessedly wonderful news about this is that it is never too late to begin. There is no place that is not the perfect place to begin, since the only directive, in practicing magic, is to begin where you are at. Begin, and practice.

Incalculably massive Mountains will soon become nothing more than a series of manageable steps, once the novice has decided which peak to summit—she has only the task of choosing which peak to summit[60]!

Socrates said that "*the unexamined life is not worth living,*" and the editor would like to suggest that what he meant was, "pay attention, so that your life is good." In beginning to actively pay attention, you practice the first steps of magical living. "*Keep[s] alive the sense of wonder by showing familiar things in an unfamiliar light[61].*" Through the practice of actively paying attention to the thoughts, the novices begin to see her way of thinking in new light. She is filled with wonder and delight at what she finds: that she is, in fact, in control of her destiny. And it all begins in practicing the art of paying attention to the thoughts in the mind: mindfulness.

A practitioner of mindfulness, her thoughts are one of three main areas of mastery (alongside communication and empathy). They are her own, and she is in full control of their content; understanding fully that "A man is what he is because of the dominating thoughts which he permits to occupy his mind." (Napoleon Hill surely included

---

[60] Cross-reference to "occupation," for advice on this line.
[61] Bertrand Russell (1872-1970)

women in his thinking; "man" is our race.) Success belongs, and flows naturally, to our modern witch.

Practical application, 001

The sub-conscious mind is merely the thoughts that we ignore, and, usefully, we may train ourselves to pay active attention. Those thoughts are the ones that we use to "order" us as we like (reference to choosing your own orders/direction/et cetera); the sub-conscious mind is the language we use to speak directly with the energetic flow of magic present within. Once the novice begins to exercise this useful tool, she will rapidly advance in all of her other practices, regardless of the previous success (or lack of) in the practiced control of magic.

The mind shapes the reality being perceived by the individual.

Magical individuals get to actively write their stories, shaping their reality; those who choose to let others write their stories, are subject to becoming characters, or puppets, under the direction of another. This is fine if the novice is a film actress, and she is following a script and being directed on set. However, permitting another to write the story she is *actively living* is dangerous, since the witch may find herself cast in an unpleasant, or otherwise undesirable role. It is therefore imperative that the witch practice mindfulness, since, as a witch thinks, so she becomes.

Tested with Reason, 001

It's worth mentioning that the thoughts we think, the incantations we practice (see *"incantations,"* p._), will change the way that the *people* in, or around, the life of the witch interact with her. Her experience of any individual will be the experience, or performance, that she draws out of that individual. The adept witch is a wonderful director! This is how it works: through the practice of mindfulness and the use of incantations (which serve to train the mind), and changing herself, the witch has the ability to reach out and pull the strings of the universe and weave together, from the endless options of multiple parallel realities, the existence she chooses. This is magical living.

It's the subconscious mind that possesses the faculty to speak directly to the old gods (the universe, the flow of energy, et cetera), and therefore, the novice has only to train her subconscious mind to realize her desired outcome. Once the subconscious believes, the threads of that optional parallel universe are woven into what we call *present reality*. And this is how the witch creates her own reality.

The training of the subconscious mind is a matter of tying up some threads as well. She must focus her energy on the most vital aspects of what she wants, or she will discover that her energy is spread all over the place, and her desired outcomes aren't being delivered in a satisfactorily speedy manner. Being even more curious than her feline familiar, the witch may require some time/energy simply in mastering the task *of focusing on only one thing at a time*. Now, she may focus on five different things throughout her day (and every day is, recall, today), but when she is focused *in the moment*, her attention will be completely occupied with that thing. This is how she effectively begins to transform energy into tangible matter, or, put more simply, begins to realize her dreams.

The sub-conscious mind is a little bit tricky until the novice begins to really understand how it works in relations to the magical flow of energy that she uses to create her reality. Let's think about this with a test of reason.

Tested with reason, 001

Here is a lesson that many will understand (the editor included!). Do you have a sweet tooth, novice? The editor recommends that you either eradicate it, or keep whatever it is that satisfies your sweet tooth handy. And this is why: when you eat your meal, or your snack, or whatever it is you are eating, and then you think, "*I need something sweet, to finish this off.*" You are telling your energy that you have *need*. The magical energy possessed by the witch is a powerful force, and it attracts *more* energy harmonizing with that which is present in the witch. When you start looking around the kitchen, or the menu, for a sweet to satisfy your *need,* you have, quite innocently, opened the door in your mind, and in your magical flow of energy, to *need*. Since energy is attracted to harmonizing energy, the novice will begin to *attract more need*. The energy she is sending out, is *calling more need*. Saying that she needs more money, needs more of *anything,* the novice is asking for, and will received, more need. So, nip that in the bud, and focus that energy on satisfaction. On noticing how much abundance you have. How happy you are that your sweet tooth will be satisfied when you eat that slice of cheesecake! *So, let's recap:*

- I *need* something sweet to satisfy our craving—draws more "need" energy, and it will do it in an endless cycle, and it will quickly devolve from a slight craving to a binge, and then a steady realizing of how much more you "need" in every other area of life.

- Think, or say, instead, it would be nice to have... this or that. "I will be so pleased with a sweet snack!" Begin a new cycle, where you are satisfied and full filled, and everything you want, you have.

- Or, even better, get used to thinking and speaking like this: "I'm so glad I have... this or that." "Calling it" the way a pool-player calls the corner pocket. Then your energy will begin to attract energy that harmonizes with *having what you desire.*

Being in tune with magic

The witch is at home in her body, which lives in the physical realm, but she is also at home in *her mind.* This is good to know, and understand, because it will help the novice to put to use the wonderful magic available to her.

The flow of energy that the witch employs—magic—is much like a dog or a horse. This makes sense if you understand how powerfully sensitive these two animals are to the *intentions* of the people around them. You may speak or say whatever you like, but it's what you are feeling that these animals respond to. A feeling, even tension in the body, is immediately sensed, and acted upon, by these creatures. This helps to explain why girls love horses, and boys love dogs, so very much (and vise-versa). It is because their energy *matches* up, and it feels good to both of them. The horse senses that the admiration and love of the little girl, and the horse feels safe and happy; there is trust between them. When that little girl learns to ride, their communication lines might get mixed up for a little while (if there's any fear in the little girl), but this is quickly remedied with practice (of riding, and regaining the trust and love between the two). The same for boys and their dogs.

This is a useful analogy, because if you can begin to think this way about your magical gift, you have a tool for understanding what you may do. To practice what this feels like, perhaps spend some time with one of these two animals, and you will discover the *easily evidenced truth* of this fact. The dog is morally neutral, but it responds to the energy of its owner. Here's an example. A large, fierce dog may, on the end of the leash of an adult male, growl and strain at an adult male passerby, while the same dog will wag its tail and whine for attention at a small child passerby. How the owner feels about the people (or the world in general) around them is *channeled* by the dog. So the magic of the witch. The energy which flows through her flows regardless of her choice to control it. The energy is there, and it's working. It is easy to use, although sometimes we benefit from learning, and training ourselves to use it. And like the dog or horse, *it is anxious to get going*!

(Check language clarity)

When the novice *fully grasps this*, she is well on her way to adept.

Feelings are the easiest way to determine whether you are living magically. Use the following parameters to determine if you are living magically, and perform the adjustments required, if any...

Feelings present which indicate effective magical living include:

1. Desire

2. Faith

3. Love/Romance/Sex

4. Hope

5. Enthusiasm

"Luck" is when opportunity meets preparation. Prepare your mind, and the rest will follow.

All of these feelings promote magical living. Ask yourself, do I feel any of these things? And if the answer is negative, then simply shift your feelings to one or more of the above. This can be performed by performing an action that changes your state, such as:

Interacting with your familiars (cat, or other)

Using auto-suggestion to plant positive emotions in the subconscious

Attending to some unmet physical desire (thirst, hunger, exercise)

Attending to some unmet spiritual desire (expressing gratitude, meditation, visualization)

Sometimes, following your "good feeling" will seem to lead you away, or on a side-path from whatever your end objective is. However, they key to ensuring that you are following the right path is to *follow* that good feeling. Doggedly working away at something, when your instincts tell you to do something else, will get you to the desired outcome, however, you will get to the desired outcome more quickly if you follow inspiration, wherever it leads, especially when it seems to lead off-track. The key is that you follow your inspired thoughts. It is important to understand this, and to practice this principle. The principle is following those feelings (listed above), where they take you. The *end result* is what the novice practitioner must focus on, opportunities will present themselves during the steps in the journey. Focusing on an outcome is how we summon into existence everything and anything we want (see, "incantations," and "summoning," p. _). Try and enjoy the journey as you move towards your desired outcomes[62]. They will become reality more quickly if you are able to develop the habit of doing this.

---

[62] When we have the urge to go outside and train the ivy, we do it, and we do it as long as it feels good to do so, even if we have a deadline (real or imagined) in our "work." But we know, from experience, that if we feel the inclination to train ivy (or mulch the garden bed), then the hour or so we spend doing this will actually *increase* our productivity in our "work" when we return to it. This is a surprising fact, but we can tell you, it is absolutely true. Follow your enthusiasm; if you enthusiasm is for training ivy, then, by golly, train ivy when the impulse strikes you.

Living in the Magic of Life:

The universe wishes to deliver, to the magical souls, the Magic of Life. The Magic of Life can be most simply described as living your fantasy life (different for each magical being). Thoughts become things: so, by thinking of

The things that give pleasure, inspiration, delight, and the magical may live a life filled with these things. There is no time frame associated with receiving the magic of life, or living magically—the only limits are the limits the witch places on herself. She

Fear is one of the biggest enemies of magical living. It's easy to conquer, however. Merely disregard it.

is, regardless of her age, or mastery of gifts, limitless. Limitless! When she understands and embraces this fact, she will begin to live magically. The ideal state for every witch. Witches may choose to live either in the magic of life, or they may choose to live in darkness, which leads, at minimum, to personal unhappiness. Such a witch may also negatively affect those around her.

Tested with Reason, 001

A note on "good" witches and "bad" witches: the difference between the good witch and the bad witch is simple: the presence of love—expressed by the witch, and given to the witch—determines whether she practices in light or in darkness. The good witch gets more satisfaction from her efforts, more bang for her energetic buck: the results in relation to the effort paid is much larger when the energy is positive, an indisputable fact. The witch who works ill, works ill in greatest measure in her own life. It is hard work for petty "satisfaction," and this creates, within the witch, a downward spiral of misery and destruction. Who wants to be that witch?

The good witch may create her own happiness, and she may generate, if she is

"know-how" is a useful foundation, but useless until it is put into practical use: practice.

talented, happiness in others through a variety of outlets. Creative outlets are frequently chosen, for their capacity to touch the largest possible audience[63], and should be considered by the witch first in choice of life work or occupation. The witch has abundant talent, and will desire to share that talent with as great a number of persons as possible.

Talent can be thought of something like the genie in Aladdin's lamp; that genie is so grateful to get out of the lamp, that it will *grant you whatever you wish*. What is your talent? What do you love? Practice doing what you love, and that "genie," released, will deliver either steps towards the witch's desired outcome, or the outcome itself.

"Somewhere in your make-up (perhaps in the cells of your brain) there lies sleeping the seed of achievement which, if aroused and put into action, would carry you to the heights such as you may never have hoped to attain[64]."

There is an abundance of magical energy present in the world we share—the good witch understands how to tap into this abundance, and draw it into herself, her life, her work, and the world around her (her audience). The larger the audience, the greater the abundance of all good things.

It's important for the witch who is beginning to practice magical living, to remember to live and practice magic before sharing the magic with others. Mastery first, then acolytes. Acolytes will come, and some will come early, and must be handled with extreme gentility and care. While the witch learns new arts and practices, her potency will greatly affect the energy of those she connects with. Power is limitless, and using her power to do good will be her continuous practice. Gratitude is the key, followed by kindness, in achieving true Good Witch status. Few fully master these two essential traits, and they should be the goal of any practicing witch, regardless of her other work.

Sometimes, a useful idea or lesson will come from an unusual source. Remember, sometimes treasure is hidden in a cave, or even in

---

[63] Many witch's enjoy an audience, and possess the capacity to give (whatever their gift may be) in an endless supply, to a very large number of people.

[64] Hill 64

a rubbish heap. Take the lessons and the ideas as they come to you, and if they inspire, take it as a gift from the source of origin.

See "Creating Reality" for more in-depth analysis.

The good witch will quickly discover, when she begins practice, that she is faced with forces of evil[65]. Take heart—such forces are easily overcome the moment she recognizes that she is, in fact, in a battle; it's barely worth mentioning, like a fly buzzing by; but since the novice may be just beginning to practice using the abundant supply of power at her fingertips, the editor feels compelled to mention it.

There is a childishly simple method for dismissing forces of evil: *ignore them.*

This directive may, at first, appear overly simple; so we will shine another light on the situation. Every person, whether magically inclined or otherwise, has *demons.* We all have demons. The hordes of hell are never far away or far behind. We may try and run from them, from place to place, from relationship to relationship, but the only way to conquer them is to acknowledge them and face them. This is easy to do once we understand that there is no spiritual equivalent for the opposite of demon. Are you plagued by your demons? Why not, instead, be plagued by their opposite? The reason that we have no word or label for the opposite spiritual effect or presence is that each and every demon possesses two faces—there are two sides to every coin. The demon we call Fear has another face: Love. Demand that your demons show the face that you wish to see, and they will obey. Every demon has another face, and until you call that face forward, it will only show you its gruesome face. Take charge, and those demons will reliably report for duty.

Every demon will submit to your directive: insist that they put their best faces forward.

---

[65] forces of evil include, and may be summoned by the name, fear (of any variety), guilt, worry, anger, et cetera. they sometimes sneak in through disappointments or setbacks. The trick to conquering the forces of evil (or darkness, or negativity) is to combat them with their more powerful flip-side. There are "coins" of energy, and every coin has two sides: love and fear share a "coin," purity and shame (embarrassment or guilt) share a coin, faith and worry share a coin, and so on. When that little fly buzzes by, simply identify which coin it is, and flip it until you get a satisfactory result.

The Imagination.

Increase your imagination, and increase your reality. Not as a one-time feat, but as a continuous practice. Increase is a state of being, and if you can imagine that, you will live that reality. How does this work?

The imagination is that most magical of faculties; when well developed, like a muscle, it is both strong and useful[66]. The imagination is that thing that the witch will earn to call upon to answer her every want or desire. It is that thing that will reliably provide the answers to every question. Used in conjunction with self-discipline, and given energetic power by the will (choice—choosing to do), there is nothing that a well-developed imagination cannot achieve for the practicing witch. While there are other functional components to "getting something done," the imagination provides the answer. Once the witch has the answer to her question, problem, or concern, she may take action to change her situation—to alter her reality.

A firm grip on reality is useful in waking life; however, an adept witch takes every opportunity to fly in her dreams.

If you can imagine it, you can create it.

It is the fundamental starting point to all change, and it occurs, takes place, in the mind. Imagination, in the mind, gives birth to ideas that are powered by action; this is how the witch transmutes energy into matter. It's wonderful magic, the best kind of magic, and the sooner the witch learns the art, and puts it into practice, the sooner her reality begins to reflect her ideals, her desired outcome.

The novice is limited by only one thing: the capacity and quality of her imagination. Begin by identifying a desire in the abstract; doing this may lead to wishing, and to hoping that chance or luck will deliver to the witch her desires. The adept practitioner practices using her imagination. Imagination prepares the soil of the mind to receive the object of desire. The modern witch understands, and harnesses,

---

[66] Inspiration comes to the practitioner who actively exercises her imagination.

this power of imagination. Anything she can imagine, she can bring to life, and she can do so in a time period specified by her own will. This sounds stupendous, impossible to believe; yet even now some readers are nodding in agreement. All but the most magically deficit are adept in this power, though those who regularly practice are the most effective. (Under mindfulness, cross referenced with gifts). Fervently desire the object of your focused imagination, and *believe that you will possess what you desire.*

The modern witch is blessed in many ways: particularly in the fact that she is whatever she imagines herself to be. Her imagination is fertile, creative, and big. As the author of her life story, she will, often, imagine and accomplish great feats.

How big is your imagination, acolyte witch? What can you imagine? It will come to you. The things that you spend your time imagining, in detail, in the present tense, will come to you. They key is releasing them in a time frame that you can (emotionally) handle. The universe will give you what you are emotionally prepared to deal with; a bold statement, yet true (in the case of adult witches).

When you are prepared to receive the thing that you are asking for, it will deliver itself to you. Take care to imagine your desires "in the present," so that they will presently become so.

practical application, 001

Imagine that you are a great actress, and you have been cast in the role of a lifetime. What would that role entail? Do you become a famous chef? Do you start your own business? Is your "film" a romantic comedy, an inspirational film, or is it drama? The delightful truth is that you have been cast in the role of a life time, and you are the writer, editor, director, and star of your own life. Imagine what you want your "role" to be, and when you really admit to yourself what that it, you'll begin to get it. Take courage, and dream as big as your imagination will take you.

Focus on what you want, and all the distractions will disappear. Sustained focus will show you the first steps towards transforming your dream roll into your waking life.

It is through the imagination that the witch is able to directly communicate with the old gods (the universe, or whichever name suits the individual witch). Her ability to imagine lifts her above the noisy cloud of thoughts present on the surface of this plane of existence, and imagination has the ability to raise the novice, like a magic carpet ride, above. From such a position, she can begin to see with new clarity, and make informed, aware decisions about where, when, and how she directs her outflow of energy.

After developing the habit of imagination, she may find that she runs into the *new ideas* that happen to be present in that plane. These delightful ideas serve to fuel imagination to greater heights.

(See also, "Summoning" p._)

Empathy (and being an Empath)

Although there exist a litany of gifts any resourceful witch may poses, let's focus on those few that have the greatest impact, or potential impact, in the life of the witch. The gift of empathy, of being an Empath, is one such gift.

This is one of those gifts that will, in all likelihood, be present in the life of the witch long before she has woken to her powers, and while it is a useful gift, it may also be a challenging gift to live with and use. Like any of the gifts, acceptance that she has it, and practice of it will be of great use to the witch. Living as an Empath means that the novice has the sometimes uncomfortable ability to resonate with the feelings of those around her, to feel their feelings acutely. When the witch experiences this, she may, if unpracticed, absorb all the feelings of the people and the world around her, and become a reactionary creature. This is a highly uncomfortable way of living, as both ourself, and a handbook beta tester[67], will confirm. Empathy is a great gift, as it can be practiced into an effective tool in the witch's belt. The witch herself is much like a mirror, and she may, once she understands her gift, reflect emotions back as well as take them in (she is, essentially, a two-way mirror). Once she learns this, she may approach a person or group, and *change their mood*. She does this by focusing her energies on a powerful feeling, and *seeing that feeling reflected onto the persons around her.* As those people begin to see themselves through her eyes, which happens in a matter of moments for all but a very few, they begin to believe that they *are what she*

---

[67] Because the editor is so whole-heartedly dedicated to sound testing methods for the practices outlined in the hand-book, during the handbook's compilation, she recruited multiple beta-testers, so that their combined results could be evaluated. The editor speaks, in the above instance, to the beta tester and friend, Freya.

sees. They are who they think she sees them as, which is wonderful, because she *sees all of the good in them*: they perform, and become what and who she sees them as, wonderful director that she is, and they will behave accordingly. They feel her energy resonating, and they say to themselves, "yes, I am that. I feel that way." Empathy is a powerful gift, and it is a great tool for fostering healing and building community.

Communication

Communication is another tool for the witch to master, now that she has awakened to magic. It is organized just after Empathy because communication is so closely tied to empathy, and it is the link between empathy and speech, which is, perhaps, the most powerful tool of all.

Taking the energetic flow of feeling in from the persons and world around is like allowing a stream to pass through the mind (soul/spirit), and the mind is a sieve which filters out the things worth keeping from those things that must be permitted to pass through. All manner of thoughts and feelings will pass though, and are of no concern to the witch. Only the things that are permitted to stop and stay, shall we concern ourselves. Those things that stop and stay build the reservoir from which the witch draws. Those are the things that she uses and puts back into the world, through the art, and practice, of communication.

Tested with Reason, 001

Pay alert, wakeful attention to what you allow to "stop and stay," because it is those things that you will communicate back to the world around you, and once you begin adding speech to that communication, you are creating a powerful energetic force: you are, quite simply, *generating reality.*

Speech

"Those who control their tongues can also control themselves in every other way.[68]"

"And if anyone does not offend in speech [never says the wrong things], (she) is a fully developed character *and* a

---

[68] James 3:2 NLT

perfect (woman), able to control (her) whole body *and* curb (her) entire nature.[69]"

Speech, in addition to being what is (perhaps) the most powerful tool, is also a sharp weapon and deserves to be handled as such: with mastery. Bridling the tongue is easier than bridling a horse, and once done, it is quite easy to rein and direct. Only say those things which you believe to be true, since the things that you say will follow you home like hungry strays[70]. Idle speech is most dangerous to the novice who permits it.

Mastering the thought life is the first step in active practice of magical living, because it is where speech begins. Speech is, simply put, the act of allowing the thoughts of your subconscious mind exit into living, pulsating reality. the conscious mind has the ability to filter these thoughts before they exit the body, and this is where mastery comes in. reality is a stew cooked up through the combination of the thoughts permitted to linger in the mind, and the speech permitted to leave the body and *come to life* in reality. Words come to life, dear novice, and they follow a set pattern: thought, speech, action, *reaction*. Reality *reacts*, responds, and *delivers* the results of the thoughts, speech, and actions of the novice and the adept. Conquer fear[71], and begin to practice mastery over your speech. You are well on your way to fulfilling all of your hearts desires when you begin this practice.

Tested Empirically, 001

The art of magical living could be summed up any number of ways, and one of those ways is the following: magical living begins when you translate the free flow of the subconscious from the ether, back out into the "real" world. You must learn to trust yourself first, and that's a matter of educating yourself. You can trust that what comes out is what you believe to be true; the beauty is this—you can do your own research to find out what you believe to be true, and you can trust the instincts of your subconscious for most of the

---

[69] James 3:2 Amplified Bible

[70] Anyone who has known a hungry stray cat also knows that they can be very bold. They will follow you home, into your home, and take over, if you permit them to. The editor experiences the problem of frequently finding strange cats in her home, and always shoo's them out with a firm, "by invitation only!"

[71] Fearlessness is a direct result of living in peace with all kingdoms.

rest. We encourage and exercise the free flow of our own subconscious, however, we are also an adamant empirical tester (having a great love for the wonder of the natural universe and its laws). And so, therefore, test evidences before permitting outflow. *Writing* is one of the ways in which one might process and regulate the flow from the unconscious. To more quickly, simply state: recapture the wonder and innocence of childhood, and allow it free reign. It will surprise and delight you, as it has been through the education process, through a school of thought, or the autodidactic habits of the practitioner.

Part Two Recap

- The seat of emotions

- Relationships

- The mind

-

Part Four: Spiritual Reality

Energy, Manipulation of

The more (frequently) the novice calls on some object or desire, the more quickly that thing responds to her call. This is, quite simply, a matter of respect for the thing that the witch calls, and for the witch herself. The witch who receives without an energy exchange also receives a dose of laziness. Laziness may lead to the neglect of practice, and the magically gifted are the best, the happiest, when they practice! Keeping those muscles stretched and ready to go, the novice is a happy, positively energetic creature. It's imperative that the natural born witch begin practice quickly, so that she does as little damage as possible to the people and the world around her.

For the non-magical, practice will add greatly to the quality of life—the curious daughter of Eve may live magically without possession of the magical heritage, and they will become just as efficient and happy of their magical friends.

Magical Energy exists and it may certainly, and easily, be transformed. The practicing witch is blessed to be a native transformer of energy[72]. However, even the natural must practice the gift, and those without natural talent for energy transformation may practice the art and become adept.

The method of practice works[73]; the practitioner may fail—and this bears repetition. Energy may be transmuted and manipulated; it works in every time, place, and through any person who chooses to embrace the practice.

Persistence is a useful key, but it must be back up with belief to open the door.

---

[72] After "waking" to magical living, the novice may view past events in new light—she may discover that magical energy assisted her at different times of testing throughout her life. This is always a pleasant and delightful discovery.

[73] Your devoted editor has put the principles to the test, and happily provides supporting third-party evidence to the truth of this fact.

Healing

The body wishes to heal itself of any and all disease and ailment. These afflictions are merely outward manifestations of inner turmoil or improper ways of thinking (stress, worry, negativity, anger, bitterness, et cetera). Disease is cured by replacing the underlying inner conflict, and can be performed by any individual, with or without the aid of the witch. However, many mortals lack the understanding to effectively cast off disease, and should consult with the healer of their choice, whether witch or physician. Both serve an important role in healing, though healing through the energy of the mind may be achieved without unpleasant side effects.

The gift of healing is practiced by following the guide of kindness. With kindness as a guide, using empathy to determine application, healing naturally flows outward. It's carried in the intention of the practitioner, and can be transmitted to the afflicted through touch, through verbal communication, or through food. Through touch, healing is given through massage, or arts such as acupuncture. Stress and other mental afflictions, in addition to muscular afflictions, may be relieved in this way. Through verbal communication the healer can administer relief to all forms of mental stresses or afflictions. Through food, the healer may heal the physical body of many ailments.

Other gifts, and the cost & benefit of,

Languages

Any witch knows well how to talk to children, most witches can communicate with animals, some others plants; really, any language our modern witch wishes to master is quick subject to her mastery. She might, on a whim, learn a new language just to offer a new friend or lover an unusual, and priceless, gift.

Speaking new tongues unlocks a door in the mind, and it releases an energy which infuses the other practices with fresh life. While any dedicated practice will yield results, this particular practice is especially awakening.

Remember, good witch, that there is a price to pay for everything. Newton's laws teach us that for every action there is an equal and opposite reaction. Gratitude is an excellent way to pay for many of the things that you desire. Sharing of gifts and talents are also suitable payment. (The darker requests require more ominous payment, and create opportunities for the criminal justice system to perform its function).

Creating Reality, Perception of Reality

The mind

We said earlier *Imagination is the ability to use language in an alternate reality*

Regardless what you believe, what you believe becomes true. Our subconscious mind directs our perception of reality, and our reality is that which we perceive. If you can learn to feed your subconscious mind on thoughts and feelings that are positive (that make you feel good) you will begin to have the power to create your own reality. *Don't fight the outside world to change your reality; change your reality from the inside.*

Life is a dream: pinch yourself, if you have to, and wake up. You are in charge of this dream.

Every living thing has a *master*. If you are a human, magically gifted or otherwise, your master lives inside your brain. Now, the novice learns to train her mind—to master her master, so to speak—however, she will greatly benefit from having an alliance with one of her like-minded magical sisters. When magical sisters (or a like-minded man with the magical heritage) sets their minds on the same goal, they are capable of achieving *literally anything*, so long as they both are able to visualize the same thing. That thing, when they imagine it together (think back upon the thoughts of the Disney princess Jasmine), they effactually create a new reality where that idea exists. Once those two accomplish that, they may then spread that reality further—they may translate it from pure energy into physical matter. Even better if the witch has several

111

such sisters! The only thing that matters is that they are of like mind on some topic of importance, and every difference between them will merely be learning opportunities. While it is the habit of the curious witch to "learn things the hard way," she may, when she has found a like-minded magical sister, learn from this sister. When the novice practices this ability, she will find herself learning at an above-natural place.

Begin immediately to put this information to useful, practical test. And above all else, *do not give up.*

Checking the evidences: there will be moments when you feel overwhelmed with the responsibility that you have taken on, or you may feel like you're going crazy—especially if you have not yet curated the companions in your life. The way that you are thinking and acting will seem contrary to the ways of thinking and acting in the people around you. In these moments, it's important to check the evidences. Look at the evidences that will begin to appear in your life: are there positive results? Has there been forward movement towards your goal? At first the evidences may be small, but

Keeping the Ship on Course: There may be moments where you feel crazy as you begin to practice your gift; in these moments, take the time to *"check the evidences."*

remember: even the greatest creatures on earth begin as tiny collections of cells banded together. Focus on those positive evidences, and *keep the ship on course.* If you have set your desired outcome, your destination, you will arrive. Like Odysseus, the Hero of the Trojan War and star of the Odyssey, you may occasionally feel lost at sea, distracted by Sirens, or even by the gods. Keep your desired outcome in mind, and you will arrive at it, whatever it may be.

Edits below

Your thoughts are your master; it benefits the novice to practice control over thinking processes. This principle is so important, that it bears repeating throughout the sections of this text. Believe in yourself, first. If you can suspend disbelief, you will be free to try, and once you try, the evidences of success of your attempts will begin to pile up. As this occurs, your confidence will grow, and you will, over time, and through practice, traverse from novice to adept.

The only limits to what you may perform or accomplish are those that are set by your own mind[74].

Controlling the contents of your mind, your thinking, is quite simple, with practice. It is as easy as identifying when you feel positive.

Tested Empirically, 001

Many years ago, we learned about currency from an expert. When a person who is trained to handle cash money, they are trained only to recognize the feel of *real* money. Real money will feel different, depending on how old, or worn, or crumpled, or dirty it may be, but it, in all of these states, feels like *real money*, because it is. This way, when counterfeit currency comes into the hand of such a well-trained person, it will be *instantly* recognized for what it is: counterfeit. Focus on what you want to be real, and instantly recognize and toss out the counterfeit.

Thinking about the things that you wish to experience, whatever they may be, make you feel good. You may train your mind by repeating, aloud (at first), the object of your desire. Whether that be education, career, wealth, love, or any other abstract or physical want you may have. Repeat aloud what you wish to have, and allow yourself the simple pleasure of believing that that thing is true. When you are ready to receive that thing, it will come to you.

We get to decide what to do with all of the information that enters our sensory perception. Use these interruptions as "check points" to examine whether you are feeling positive—living magically.

Supply your subconscious mind with your "order" and your subconscious mind will translate the order in the *tense* of the order (use present tense!). Your order will be delivered to you in the tense the order was made, once that order has been "translated" into the

---

[74] This is a bold statement, but one that the editor feels confident relaying to the reader.

language of magic. Sometimes it may benefit the novice to use the helpful tool of "incantation" which is something like placing the order with definite clarity. Communication lines are sometimes fuzzy! Make sure that the order is clear. Delivery of the desired outcome is related only to the witch's belief in the difficulty, or the size or scope of the order itself. It's a matter of making sure the order is clear, and the training of the subconscious mind (often against its natural state of processing) that you are capable of receiving the order which you have placed. However, once you have convinced your subconscious mind of your belief, your subconscious mind will supply the rest of whatever your desired outcome is.

The road chosen is the pleasure of the individual witch (Robert Frost Quote), only focus on the end result of what you wish to receive or achieve, and the journey will be delightful, whether she chooses the high road or the low. The end result will be delivered to you, if you can free yourself from obsessing over the details of the journey itself. Enjoy the journey. Remember, it's the in-between moments that count.

Conquering Fear

Energy may be manipulated by the witch, and she does so in two major capacities: manipulating energy (the basic principles, and hardest to master), and through the manipulation of energy, manipulating a specific end result—matter. Some energy manipulation results in intangible matter manipulation (such as healing an illness or relieving worry and stress), and these will be addressed in the first section, "Energy, manipulation of," as well as basic understanding of the process of manipulating energy. In the second section, "Matter, manipulation of," we will address those specific visible physical outcomes that may be manipulated by the witch who has use of her gifts.

Power is in our fingertips; learn to recognize your own hands, and allow them to do what they were designed to do (we innately crave the thing that we were designed to do—it's a self-regulating system). We each have our own desires, and there is more than enough for all who have the courage to *ask for what they want.*

How would you behave, if all your hopes and dreams came true? If you had the amount of money you wish you had, the career you wish you had, the partner you wish you had? Behave as if you already have them. Practice feeling what it feels like to have these things. When they come to you, you will know what to do with them, and how to enjoy them.

As a witch, you give birth to reality.

The sixth sense: Telepathy, clairvoyance

Choose carefully what you incubate.

All witches possess the faculty of the sixth sense, which encompasses telepathy, and clairvoyance, among other potentialities, whether she actively uses the sense or ignores it. It is our aim to

deliver for your benefit the most basic, practically useful information for the practice of magical living, and so we will only briefly engage on what is, realistically, a very large topic. That we possess a sixth sense can be taken on reason, and it can be tested empirically; and thank goodness! It is a key with which the novice may unlock any door that she can imagine. Having already learned how to use her imagination, and practicing the incantations (which, while reading this, the novice has begun to learn to do—take heart, it will come quickly), the novice has effectively learned the language to use to *make known her desired outcome*. She speaks to her own energy in its native tongue, and that energy gets to work bringing her what she desires (part of the importance of being clear on your desire is that it must bear translation into this other *tongue*; clarity will ensure that the language survives translation). Once she has made clear her desires, and submitted the information to the energetic flow of magic present within herself, *that energy responds*. It responds in a variety of forms, and each and all may be useful to the resourceful novice. Most easily, and most obviously, she receives back, from her energy, inspiration, or a "hunch" about something. She will feel delighted at the *good idea* that has sprung into her mind from... out of the ether. If it is a new thought, to her, then it did, indeed, come from the ether—it was delivered to her through her magical heritage. And this works for small detail, such mundane operations as working a coffee pot, to the occupation of her energy (her life's work). A quick note on occupation of energies, related to "work." The work will, if it is what it should be, make the witch profoundly happy, and it will require that she constantly drawn on this sixth sense. It becomes something bigger and better than her best, which is what makes it *magical*. And it can be anything from being teaching piano to being an A-list actress.

practical application, 001

By continuously using this faculty, the novice begins to effectively act on her "orders." Remember, these are the orders that she has chosen for herself, and they are relevant to the overall "order" which she has chosen (remember the analogy of the orders of catholic nuns?). This is why it is so important to choose your own order, so that you will receive "orders" that you will *enjoy carrying out*. If the novice is unsatisfied with the orders she is getting in her life, then she should choose a new order.

Each of the faculties of the sixth sense are an expression of the energy that passes through us, and which, if we practice, we may harness. Electricity is an excellent example of harnessing energy, and we use electricity daily—reliably. We use it, we pay our electricity bills. It comes to us after being generated (captured) through a process.

We know how electricity functions, and we understand that electrical particles behave, that there are equal numbers of positive and negative particles... when these particles form and make bonds, *matter* comes into existence. Clusters of particles form atoms, and "where two or more atoms...form a molecule... and when trillions of molecules combine... form a speck of matter (Hewitt 410-411).

tested with reason, 001

Act as if each person you encounter *can, in fact*, read your mind, or your thoughts. You will be surprised to discover that people respond to your thoughts much more often than you may have previously realized.

If it is true that we first create our reality in our minds, and that reality is then expressed in tangible matter, the sort of stuff that we may, if we choose test empirically, then we should be aware of what and how we are thinking when we are in the presence of our friends, or co-workers, or other companions. If you feel dislike for someone, and you think that is a secret from that person, you are incorrect. We think that we are smarter than dogs? Or other "lower" animals? Even a dog may communicate without words. To suggest that we would have lost such an important trait, in an upward evolution, is nonsensical at very best, and it is an insane assumption at worst.

Let us think about this a moment, and return, again, to the analogy of the dog (or horse, which is another highly sensitive, highly in-tune animal). We use language with the dog, or other animal or familiar, but most persons, whether they have had a familiar of their own, has, at some point or another in their lifespan, experienced that way that an animal responds to their *mood.* The dog, the cat, the horse, the familiars that witches keep close to hand, they are all sensitive to the mood of the novice. The novice may speak conforting words, or use peaceful gestures, and if those gestures calm the witch, they will also calm the animal; it is a combination of the intention and the words or gestures that the animal picks up on. This is preciscely is why having a familiar is *so important* for the practicing witch. The familiar allows the witch to see, test, practice, and respond to what she learns by paying attention to her familiar. Even if the novice is unaware of her own mood, or feelings, the familiar is *acutely aware.* By learning to pay attention to the familiar, the novice may take steps towards becoming better at identifying the moods within herself, and more effectively create her own reality. No witch wants to feel unhappy, grouchy, angry, disappointed, sad, or any other of the associated negative crew of feelings. Like any person, magical or non-magical, the witch desires to feel good.

We pretend that we can't understand each other, and this causes much miscommunication. Think the thoughts that you are comfortable with each person hearing, and think the thoughts about what you want to happen when you are around a person or group of people. You will find that you are able to positively influence both people and events, if you practice harnessing the power of your thoughts. You will also require less speech, which can be, if the novice allows it, empowering.

More on this.

Mental telepathy—sometimes the presence of a person is enough to dampen the mood, or cause the novice to feel insecure, or any number of other negative feelings associated with bad energy. The witch certainly attracts all sorts of energy (energy likes to band together in groupings—this is why a party either reaches critical mass (if it does), there's an energy ratio to be reached), but she may also be susceptible to the telepathy of other witches, *and* daughters of Eve. The novice must learn to shut this energy out, like the front door after an impolite guest has been ejected from the home. A thought or feeling will pass directly from one mind to another, which is wonderful when the persons are in harmony with one another (and the reason it's important to surround oneself with harmonizing influences), but disastrous when disharmonious; this function, which, when good is wonderfully good, has also the potential to kill desire, kill belief, wipe out ambition and persistence, and completely shut-off the communication between the novice and the magical flow of energy present within herself (remember, it's a translation process between the witch and her energy). Guard yourself against this, witch, by putting your will power to good use—creating, effectively, a wall of immunity.

Matter, Manipulation of

The Natural World

Every atom is composed of a positively charged nucleus, surrounded by negatively charged atoms (Hewitt 411). We are, being a union of energy and matter, also composed of positively charged energy. Being surrounded by negative charges will *change* our natural internal state. Witches are neither good nor evil, as non-magical humans are neither good nor evil, in their base state. We are neutrally charged. Negative feelings (like negative electrons) buzz around in a flurry of action, they possess the same negative charge in the same amount. Positive energy, as demonstrated by protons, while at least 1800 times more massive than negative energy, as demonstrated by electrons, can be sidetracked by those tiny buggers.

The law of conservation of energy, one of the greatest generalizations in physics (Hewitt 117), says that

Energy cannot be created or destroyed; it may be transformed from one form into another but the total amount of energy never changes.

Time/Energy Harmony: Transforming intention into physical reality

As a man thinketh...

Everything that is, first began as a thought

Thoughts become things

"You create your own universe as you go along," Winston Churchill

Law of attraction, secret, N. Hill, etc.

Pure energy (perfect belief, as a result of continued perfect practice), time/energy exchange (practice exchange), currency via time/energy exchange (currency may be cash, education, or other exchange).

Mastering the manipulation of matter using time

Time is an entity, a deity; she does demands respect, and she rewards the mistresses (and masters) who pay her respect and occasional gratitude. She is kind to those who respect her, and permits them keep their vitality.

Energy changes forms, and it may be transferred from one place to another. We possess the power to transform our energy into reality.

Practical application, 001

The interesting thing about time is that *every day is today.* There is no yesterday, except in our "memories," and there is no tomorrow, except for the one that we expect, hope, or believe for—our *memories* of the future. When the novice begins to learn this, it will be as if scales have fallen from her eyes, and she is able, perhaps for the first time, to see the magnitude of power residing in her fingertips. Or words. Here is a useful tip:

Our memories and our dreams are one and the same. One looks backwards and we call it "memory," while the same faculty also looks forward, resulting in dreams and goals, or as worry and fears; however, there is *only today*. Reality exists *now*, and we generate that reality with the faculty we call memory. Inside of the novice dwells everything that she has ever been, or ever will be. She must learn to comfort and console the inner child, give that child hope, and also admire and respect the future woman who is to come; both reside within the novice, and when the novice learns to care for all three (maiden, mother, crone), she will begin to fully understand the time/energy harmony.

Time and energy being synonymous, the practicing adept is a natural time-traveler[75], and possesses, within her range of gifts, the ability to do so with ease. It is as simple as using the power we call on to relive a childhood memory, and applying that same energetic feeling to a future scenario.

Tested with Reason, 001

This is why childhood summers seemed endlessly long, and why time seems to accelerate as you get older. Because some people lose the habit of living fully the in-between moments; those are the moments where magic happens, where dreams become reality (Some "grow up faster" than others, and some "never grow up." It seems useful to the editor to grow up and learn, then return, as quickly as possible with the lessons learned, to a child-hood reminiscent state of wonder).

Time-travel to "when" you *already* *have* what you want.

[75]Since, of course, time is actually an illusion. We use time only as a *framework* with which we prepare our minds for the reality we wish to exist. Use time to your advantage, novice! "People like us, who believe in physics, know that the distinction between past, present, and future is only a stubbornly persistent illusion." - Albert Einstein

Tested empirically, 001

For the witch who desires to experience the phenomena, the editor recommends making very small steps until such time as the witch is assured she may safely return to a reality of her choosing; this is done with the careful mastery of the novice-level magic. A choice must be made, regarding this magical energy; you will feel it residing within when it is available for use.

Practical application, 001

A wonderful practical application for time travel can be thought of, or used, in the following manner: by "time-travelling" in the mind (the spirit housed within the body—the spirit may leave and go about and get business done while the body is happy and safe in its own "time") to a *time* when you already possess the thing you desire, you begin to get used to it. By moving forward in time (this type of time travel, we call it "imagination," but it doesn't matter what you call it. It is what it is, and it delivers empirical evidence, when tested), and experiencing your desired outcome *for real*, you pull that thread, of the infinite possibilities available in the multiple parallel realities that exist for us to choose from (our own story may affect the world at large—great leaders and great villains knew how to use this gift deftly), you pull that thread into the tapestry that is your life. You choose the threads, you color your existence, and you create your reality—and this is how it is done. This is a very practical application, and the editor recommends that the novice begin to immediately put it to practical test and application. The editor is confident that the novice will be delighted with the results such tests yield. The editor wishes to reiterate, to illustrate the importance of this concept: "time" travel in your imagination to the reality you wish to see evidenced around you in the *now*. You will open those pathways, those doors, and draw those threads into existence in the reality which we may test empirically.

Are you uncomfortable in a situation? Imagine living in a "time" or place, where you feel wonderful, and all the things that surround that wonderful feeling; practice this, and make a habit of doing this. Some may accuse you of being a "dreamer," or of living in a "fantasy," and for a time, it may seem that way to an outside perspective. Know this, novice—everyone who has achieved anything at all—happiness, love, wealth, all of the good things of life, by first dreaming that *they could have those good things*. Every person who wins a race is the same person that *believed that they could.*

memory

the novice witch possess the astonishing capacity to use memory to her advantage. Memory exists in three phases, much the same way that water exists in three phases, or states. Whether ice, liquid water, or steam, it's all water. Such is the reality of the witch when it comes to memory. She has the power to remember past, present, *and the future*, and she may revise these memories continuously to reflect what she wishes

It's what you do with the in-between moments that really counts.

to experience. Past memories are useful for teaching lessons, and the witch who remembers her past can use the lessons of those memories to inform the present and future memories. Present "memory" is something she can trust to auto-pilot, if she wishes, so that she may free her energy, her magic, to "remember" the future. Remembering the future is a faculty well worth developing; it is absolutely the most essential form of memory, and we'll spend some time explaining this before moving forward.

The future that you "remember" is the future you get. Do you spend time worrying about having enough in the future? Do you look forward fearfully? Afraid of being alone, of not having enough? Or do you use your energy, your future memory, to remember the future that you truly desire? What you spend your energy on is what will be delivered to you. This may seen frightening at first, but once you begin to practice and master the art of future memory, you will begin to step into the reality that you *really want.* Keep calm and cheerful, and above all else, *don't worry.*

When it comes to memory, especially memory of the future, it's vitally important that the witch get very clear on where she is going. To know what she wants, and be able to visualize it in the same way that she can travel backwards to a favorite adolescent or other past memory. Travel forward into memories of where you wish to be, and you will draw that future towards yourself. A word of advice: focus on the things that you have the power to control, and remember the lesson from Aladdin's Geni: you may not bring anyone back from the dead, you may not induce someone to love someone else. You must also work within the laws of the universe, unless it is your desire to write (or direct, or act in) science fiction or fantasy novels or films. Use your memories within the reality that exists, the shared reality, and you will be both astonished and satisfied at the results. Like the rest of the advice in the handbook, this takes practice, and it's best to build confidence with small things first, and when you discover you have become adept at this, carry on to larger things. an Additional recommendation: *remember* things spiritual and physical, so that balance is sustained. More on how to practice this art can be found under "Summoning." (cross-reference).

We know that the possibilities are unlimited, regarding future outcomes However, she chooses, in general, to only go forward, because she understands the supremacy of power can only be achieved by living completely in each moment, and selecting that moment from the infinite options available to her imagination (thus the reason for the important practice of using the imagination), that is, bringing her future to her where she is at. This factor points to the extreme importance of carefully curating her tribe (friends, hobbies, employment). It's imperative that these are positive forces, or her powers will be severely diminished.

Once you begin living magically, you may decide, when you recognize the power at your fingertips that you may manipulate time. Living with, and using time is one of our many gifts: as we mentioned above, time is an entity, and if you respect time, time will bless you and give you whatever you want. You may speed up, or slow it down, at any time you like, once you understand the principle. However, permit me to suggest that you practice enjoying each moment in between the major "plot points" of your life. This is a life well-lived.

Tested with Reason, 001

A word on "matter."

Testing through the senses is how we test empirically, and what we are testing, with those senses is "matter." Let's look at this idea another way. We live in the internet era, and what that means , practically, is that anyone may go on to a computer, access the internet, and look at pictures of items of *anything* they desire, and they may order almost any of those things *online.* We trust that those things we have ordered will

We may believe in the unseen, through the useful faculty of understanding.

be delivered to us, after we submit our payment (participate in an energy exchange). We touch those things only with our imaginations, although we understand that the image before us on the computer screen might be a photograph of the actual item we have ordered—and, even further than that, we understand that we are actual just looking at points of magnetized light, in the form of "pixels" that resolve under our eyes. We literally exchange pure energy for matter when we do this—we effectively alter our reality, by transforming energy (buying an item online) into physical matter (when it is delivered to us by the postal service, or other delivery carrier). The "internet" is an unseen force, yet we know how to use it. That is magic of a high order, and we are able to *believe in the unseen* through the useful tool of *understanding*.

To illustrate further: we live in an age where we may order practically anything online (yes, even canned air! Water! Food! We can rent a house online, too!), we live in an age where we can become *friends* with people whom we have never seen in person. We may even have correspondences over the course of years, and develop strong feelings of love, of any variety or form, for this same person who we have never seen, touched, or smelled[76].

Immortality

"... through the infinity of the universe the mind which contemplates it achieves some share in infinity[77]."

Related to time, Immortality is worth discussing at this point. Immortality is the ability to skip through time, without losing one's youth. The Modern Witch may achieve immortality at any point she chooses, but she faces a Herculean task--she must decide to accept the vessel she's in as her "forever" body (vessel, flesh, vehicle--there are many interchangeable, equally correct terms).

Immortality, cont.: those who accept it are the ones content to stay in this plane (this world) beyond the natural lifespan.

Lucifer, "Light-Bringer," (double check translation of name, the other names available), is also called the Prince of the Earth. That fallen angel became prince, and those who accept immortality (a gift we share with him, just as guests at a wedding all enjoy the same wine, dancing, and feasting, whether they are on the bride's side, or the groom's side) are consenting to stay here on Earth—his domain. Luckily, he's a good business man and understands that it takes "all sorts". Use this knowledge to your benefit; if you choose to stay, you begin to get to write your own story (script, tale, legend, history).

---

[76] The editor is particularly fond of smelling things, because you can tell quite a lot about a thing by the way it smells. It is recommended that the novice practice using this sense!

[77] Russell, 1912.

124

Those who choose to stay love the light to varying degrees; they also understand that the less time spent under the sun, the longer the evidence of the passage of time is delayed (in the body). Cool weather and shade (L'Heure Bleue), are an ideal combination.

The best (and worst) witches in history are still around (the ones who chose immortality—and many do). Just when one begins to feel neglected, as if she's been forgotten, some creative mortal will be inspired to resurrect her, whether in art, literature, film, or other communication media. In this case, our modern witch (pleural, there are many) wishes to alert the public of our existence, in a discreet, practical manner, so as to best lay the foundation for peaceful coexistence with the daughters of Eve (more on the children of Eve/Lilith later). Please enjoy the contents which have been meticulously prepared for your viewing.

Astrology and Immortality (consult Robert on this!!!)

Astrological signs and lifecycles (lives). Each magically gifted person is born, in their first life, under the first of the zodiac signs. Once the individual has mastered all the *positive* aspects of that sign (no matter how many lifecycles it takes), they will move on through to the next sign. In order to pass through each sign in the entire cycle, the lessons of the present sign, and the preceding sign, must be practiced perfectly (on the whole). A magical soul may live 12 lives, or hundreds or even thousands. It's the choice of the individual. Lives may be lived in endless repetition, but true immortality will only become available to those who master the positive traits of all the signs, and then, at the end of their cycle in Pisces, choose to continue on this plane. Those who choose to continue cycling will pass back into the matter of the universe.

Blessed indeed is the witch who remembers all her past lives, the lessons learned in them: physical, mental, and emotional.

In our first cycle through this plane of existence, we have just the smallest measure of energetic spark. As we travel through cycles of life, the level of energetic spark we possess increases. Sometimes, people with a high level of energetic spark are identified as "old souls." Old indeed.

Tested with Reason, 001

A working knowledge of evolutionary biology assists us here, and does so with pleasure: we know, with positive assurance delivered to us in the fossil record, that at least 98% of species that have ever existed on this planet are *already extinct*. And *that* is where all the souls have been drawn from in answer to the question of the human population explosion. It's also helpful to know and understand that most souls still reside in beetles, the most plentiful genus on our planet.

A note on vampires: vampires are witches who have chosen immortality; they have chosen to occasionally conceal themselves from the public eye at intervals allowing mortals to forget about them (at least for a little while).

For the witch who chooses to pass on her "ticket" to immortality, it is recommended that she learn the art of remembering *all of the previous lives* during each life cycle, so that she may learn new lessons in each life cycle, instead of re-learning the same lessons over and over again (which is exhausting to all but the most ruthlessly adventurous witches).

Finally, a simple, practical method: there is a method of immortality which has somewhat accurately been depicted in the contemporary Harry Potter novels (cite reference) as *horcruxes*. The basic idea is correct, in theory, but it need not be a malevolent force, as portrayed in the novels and the films that followed. We leave pieces of ourselves inside the people and things that we interact with. It's as if they become charged with our energy through proximity. A witch might purposefully designate "heirs" in which her essence may continue forward in time, indefinitely. These vessels may be many, of few, or none at all. Immortality may be gained in the classical sense, *kleos apthiton* (Iliad footnote reference), in either song or literature, the immortal in a sense always alive so long as their story perpetuates across media[78].

---

[78] Literature and song as well as all the contemporary options for information consumption.

Summoning

Summoning is, at its most practical, how we control the flow of magical energy that is always present in the natural witch—which, even more basically, answers the question, "how do I get stuff?."

Wherever that "stuff" resides on the hierarchy of requirements is irrelevant—whatever "stuff" the witch desires, she may acquire using the principles described and illustrated here. The less visible a thing is, the more "real" it actually is—what that statement translates to is—the less visible a thing is, the more essential to *life* that thing is (as demonstrated earlier, when we talked about air, sleep, water, food). To reiterate: the witch, novice and adept, has the tool of summoning available to draw to herself everything and anything: the most essential to the most mundane.

The witch "communicates" with the magical flow of energy within through the subconscious, and she speaks to her subconscious in the language of *feeling*. If you're feeling bad, then you are working dark magic, even if only on yourself.

Summoning is merely the fruit of the habit of persistent belief that what you focus on (receiving) will be delivered to you. Begin immediately; figure out what you want, and ask for it; summon it, and trust that it will be delivered. Imagine if you order a pizza: if you order it, it will come. We trust that this will happen. When the pizza is ordered, we go from wanting pizza, deciding to order pizza, calling in the order, to believing that it will arrive. We understand that payment must be made, and we perform an energy exchange of some variety (a series of numbers carried through wireless transmission across the ether—also known as "giving credit card information over the phone," or through cash in hand

"It would be really nice to

_____ "

Fill in the blank.

when the delivery person arrives with the pizza). The reason pizza is delivered so reliably is that we fully believe, and expect that it will be delivered to us. This is the *state of mind* you must master to successfully practice the art of summoning.

Fill the in-between moment's activities in alignment with what you are summoning. Be specific in what you summon, so that you may be happy with the fruits of your summoning.

Tested Empirically, 001

During our empirical testing of the advice recorded here in the handbook, as an example of how this works in practical reality (the stuff we see with our eyes) can be found in this vignette. Yesterday, while looking in our utility closet, we thought, "gee, wouldn't it be nice to have our air filters changed?" and today, there was a knock at our door. Naturally, we thought it would be James Franco. We were surprised to see the apartment complex maintenance man, and he said, "hi there! I'm here to change your air filters!" he was such a nice, cheerful, man; and now we have new air filters.

Summoning and Memory

The magically gifted possess the talent for remembering the past, the present, and the future. The moment when the novice learns that she *remembers everything* is a powerful moment in the history of the witch. The way that summoning and memory work together is this: if the witch can get very clear about *remembering her ideal future*, then not only will she weave that future into her present reality, her current, or residual reality, will be taken care of as well. Leave behind fretting about yesterday. Plan and manage activities each day, use your time/energy to remember your future (desired outcome).

Practical Application, 001

Here is an easy way to think about how the witch manipulates energy into matter through the process of summoning: Think about the nice things you'd really like, whether air filters or whatever else you can imagine; when you have that thought, you are experiencing the nice feeling that having that thing would bring you. Spend your energies in this way, thinking about the things that you have that you are pleased about, and the *things you want*—focus here. This creates an opportunity for an energy exchange, and as soon as you begin to think about the things that you have that you are happy about, and the things that you want that would please you, you are releasing the flow of magic to begin to work, and it *immediately goes to work for you.* The delivery may take a day, or several days—time is relative—but so long as you are in that flow of positive energy, the things that harmonize with that flow of energy will begin to present themselves to you. When this begins to happen, you will naturally feel happy and grateful, and this creates the opportirnity for it to happen more and more, until it's a continuous habit: magical living.

A word of advice on summoning: you are filled with great power, witch; it will greatly benefit you when you acknowledge it and practice it. The power resides, and it is your responsibility to decide *how* it is used, because it is *always working*—whether you choose to direct it or not. Actively wield it, and summon pleasant, desirable things. Here's a lesson from the book of Job, in the bible: *"For what I fear comes upon me, and what I dread befalls me"* *(*Job 3:25, NASB). What we like about this particular translation is that is uses *present tense*, which nicely illustrates the *power we have over what we summon.* All the higher emotions (whether love, faith, hope, or fear, dread, and despair, exist purely in the realm of *energy*; of magic. These are the tools with which we guide the outward flow of energy, and when we master the mixing of the "energetic" tools with "physical" tools, we have mastered the use of the gift. This wonderful gift of magic, and the free will to use

"Anything acquired without effort and without cost is generally unappreciated, often discredited." (Hill 99)

it, come at a price: the responsibility to wield it. It's like a powerful, energetic horse: bridle it, or it will run wild (possibly trampling and injuring its would-be handler in the process). We suggest that the novice use the gift, instead, to live magically.

Summoning is as simple as directing your focus, and holding that focus. Through this simple process, you may summon into existence anything that you choose.

It is, thankfully, much easier to summon positive things, people, and experiences than it is to summon negative ones. Negative, or darkly intentioned summoning's require substantially greater energetic effort to produce.

When summoning, focus on the desired end result. The details will work themselves out.

Soul mate

When summoning for your soul-mate, remember that there may be some delay through time and space. Persistent calling is important, because for successful pairing, both soul-mates will call for each other at the same time. To ensure that you "get each other's call," call with the level of urgency that meets your desire for speed.

Test of Reason, 001

Whatever we are wanting, we may summon, and we will get exactly what we ask for! Hurrah! Even when it comes to partners; let us take a moment to talk a little bit about soul mates. Our soul mate will come when we learn how to call back—and we try doing this *before we understand what we are doing*. This results in what can be understood as "missed call," or "wrong number" situations, which we will talk more about in a moment. But first, a practical illustrations:

By streamlining your requests for ease of delivery, you will get much more quickly to your destination and skip over much pain and heartache (for the novice and her partners). For example, if you ask for a partner who is handsome, and smart, and sexy, and talented, and funny… you will get that. And it might make you happy for a little while, but what the novice will discover is this: maybe he doesn't pay enough attention to you. Maybe he doesn't show gratitude to anyone. Maybe he, this or that. For the novice to list *every single quality* that she wants, she will find that she is devoting her energy to something which will deliver *exactly* what she has asked for. Has she asked for everything that she wants? When she is specific, her results will be specific—what this means, practically, is that if she summons 25 qualities, the partner delivered may lack the 26th quality, which she later realizes, is *very important.*

There is a wonderfully easy solution, thank goodness! Simply focus your energy on summoning your perfect partner. Your soul mate. Or, your perfect friend. What "perfect" is will mean something different to *every person.* All of the details will work themselves out, because it is the witch's *own energy* which is at work for her, and her own energy knows exactly what "perfect" is, for her. By stepping back and focusing on the most basic, most fundamental desire, the witch can get more quickly, and happily, to her desired outcome.

The witch may have a person in mind already when they begin to summon their soul mate. There is no right or wrong way to summon the soul mate, however, there is a *best practice.* If the witch truly wishes to summon her perfect soul mate, then she ought to *do just that.* Trust that the perfect soul mate will be delivered[79], and *that is what you will get.* If you desire to have a particular person, you may "have" that person for a time. If the witch continues to call her perfect soul mate, while partnered, she may find herself emotionally tied to a partner that decreases her magicality.

The art of summoning and the use of song or mantra

Tested with Reason, 001

It is our duty to recommend, having learned from personal experience, the *summoner practice consistently.* It is also our hearty advice that the summoner abandon small thinking, and think in terms of "life, the universe, and everything [80]" or,

---

[79] Again, the editor wishes to reiterate: the witch summon with *her own* energy, and if she trusts herself, she may summon exactly what she desires. She should remain open-minded, and trust that what is delivered will be perfect. Avoid, if possible, "wrong number" situations.

[80] Douglass Adams reference, cite

think of the broad, abstract things that are the source of all other subsequent desires. For example, you may ask for $25,000, but it is of much greater benefit to also be able to summon "abundant wealth." The magic happens here: A is you asking, Z is when you receive what you asked for. Just enjoy each moment between A and Z, and Z will deliver itself to you. Here's the magic: by asking, an idea or inspiration will be delivered to you which will open the door, or a series of doors, that, in a sense, "transport" you to your desired result. The novice may go the way of the poet, and choose a road— but that way is slow. Instead, go the way of science-fiction, and teleport directly—we confidently assure you, that while you are in the "transporter" (metaphorically speaking) you will be entertained to your heart's content, and feel happy and delighted. If you stop feeling good, then you've stepped out of the energetic transformational flow. There's a simple fix: step back in! You'll know when you're there, because you feel good again.

Your editor shares this fact with confidence, having previously been an expert at hopping in and out of that tractor beam.

Because we do believe wholeheartedly that this is the best path, even though the novice may choose any path that does no harm. We provide for you one of our personal "songs" for your education:

Undesirable thoughts may enter the mind; pluck them out, and carry on.

"Everything we do brings abundant pleasure and abundant wealth; abundant love and abundant health; our desires are delivered, we are always satisfied; we sleep when we will it, and rise better every time."

The novice may choose a song or a mantra, either will perform the same service. That service is to provide the witch with a pleasant release from the continuous responsibility of her thoughts. When she sings, she may pleasantly release herself into some task or another, and she effectively "kills two birds with one stone," she is shirring up her foundation, and reminding herself what her story is about, and she is occupying her physical body with the tasks of daily life, such as household chores or physical labor or exercise. Dance seems to be an additional method of serving the same purpose, and we have found it extraordinarily useful and beneficial in our own practice.

You may notice that our personal song sounds appropriate for a Disney film; the reason is this: the song is *magical*. Disney does a good job of taking snapshots of magical living, within the context of fairy tales or other folk and hero tales. We are so grateful for the Disney cartoons!

Practical application, 001

Please remember, as you practice, whether novice or adept, that your mantra must be your own words, for you to believe them, and to use them to generate the fabric of your reality.

Summoning in another light: *Prophesy* is another word for summoning, and it may be used interchangeably; it is simply the action of speaking or writing something that is afterwards supported by evidence. There follows the transmutation of pure energy into visible matter[81].

A note on summoning (footnote, or re-write for text)

Focus on readying yourself

When you are ready, the thing(s) that you desire (and that you have summoned, and that you have the imagination to believe for) will be delivered to you speedily and easily[82]. Let's look at it like preparing for a date that you are looking forward to: you have set a day, and you both know that it's either a day-date, or an evening-date, and maybe you have set a *time*. Regardless of whether you have set an exact time, it's unpleasant if your date arrives either too early (and you still getting ready), or much too late[83] (and you have to wait). Release him to arrive at just the right time by setting a date, and then *making yourself ready*. When you are ready to leave the house—to turn off the lights and walk out the door—then your date is released to arrive. He may arrive immediately, or within a short time—he likes speed too—remember, he's looking forward to this date just as much

---

[81] This concept is elegantly driven home throughout the biblical book of actions. Or Acts, which can be summed up in the following statement: *because it was written, it had to be fullfilled.*

[82] "The only reason for time is so that everything doesn't happen at once." - Albert Einstein

[83] This date doesn't cancel, or forget completely. He's a good date.

as you are. So, when you are ready, *begin*. After you have released him to arrive, through the act of readying yourself, busy yourself with your life. Yes, use the in-between moment to get something done. Action is the key to releasing your date to arrive on time. The editor practices, and recommends, such activities as sweeping the house, or vacuuming, or organizing a plan for some later course of action. He *always* arrives as soon as he is released to do so.

On quantum physics and "time"

Einstein believed, and proved, that *time is relative*. This varies from Newtonian physics, which treats "time" as an absolute value. Another wonderful, celebrated physicist, Richard Feynman, explained it something like this:

Insert quote text, & re-write and cite

Sum over Histories.

Just as Einstein's own Relativity Theory led Einstein to reject time, Feynman's Sum over Histories theory led him to describe time simply as a direction in space. Feynman's theory states that the probability of an event is determined by summing together all the possible histories of that event. For example, for a particle moving from point A to B we imagine the particle traveling every possible path, curved paths, oscillating paths, squiggly paths, even backward in time and forward in time paths. Each path has an amplitude, and when summed the vast majority of all these amplitudes add up to zero, and all that remains is the comparably few histories that abide by the laws and forces of nature. Sum over histories indicates the direction of our ordinary clock time is simply a path in space which is more probable than the more exotic directions time might have taken otherwise.

Other worlds are just other directions in space, some less probable, some equally as probable as the one direction we experience. And sometimes our world represents the unlikely path. Feynman's summing of all possible histories could be described as the first timeless description of a multitude of space-time worlds all existing simultaneously. In a recent paper entitled Cosmology from the Top Down, Professor Stephen Hawking of Cambridge writes; "Some people make a great ourstery of the multi universe, or

Using and understanding Time/Energy

When you are wondering when in "time" or how much "time" it will take for you to receive what you desire, think instead on this: use "time" as practicing *believing that you are already in possession of what you desire*. Once you believe this, which make take some "time," there may also be actions involved during this "time" period (such as steps that will help you believe that you *can* have the thing that you desire to possess), once you convince yourself that you do, in fact, possess what you desire, you have released it to come to you, and you will discover that it *has been transformed from energy into matter*.

When you want something, and you think to yourself, "I will give that more *time,*" really, all that you are saying is, *give that thing more energy.* The thing that you give your energy to is what is brought to you. The more energy you devote, the more *focused direction of time,* the more quickly that thing will materialize (rewrite for clarity in this paragraph) *So* when you spend your energy, the way that you use and divide your energy between summoning the outcomes you desire (health, wealth, a car, home, occupation, partner, et cetera), you will have delivery of the desired outcome when you *have exchanged sufficient energy to realize that desire*: to be able to sustain focus on *believing that you live in the reality where that outcome is already yours.* It's all in your hands, or, your mind, as it were. When your mind can handle that reality, is prepared to receive the object of desire, the desire will be delivered to you.

Tested with Reason, 001

Sometimes it helps to see an idea under different light: think of preparing a meal; you may have a recipe (from a cookbook our mind), and then you gather ingredients, then you combine those ingredients, you cook them, then there is the end result: a prepared meal. Which you are then able to enjoy and eat. You exchange payment in the form of time/energy (see *"time/energy harmony,"* p._) for an outcome: eating food. You may also make a phone call, and have food delivered to your home, which will require payment in the form of currency, which is given (in general practice) in exchange for time/energy at a job. Either way, there is desire (eat food), some delay (cook time/delivery time), and there is a payment in energy, though it's first degree energy when you cook at home, and second-degree energy if you pay with currency exchanged for time/energy.

While this may be hard to believe at first, it is, wonderfully, a testable practice, please be encouraged to test this practice without out ceasing! The more you practice, the better at it you become. Remember, for every desire that you request, you choose your payment—you get to choose the method, the amount, and the due-date, of that payment. You may choose to pay with belief. It is our personal recommendation, as we have mentioned elsewhere in the handbook, gratitude. This puts the practitioner in a positive place to continuously cycle the positive energy—these outlets of gratitude help to maintain hold on the desires with the highest value (love, balance, kindness, happiness; all the good feelings with which to enjoy the successes).

Tested Empirically, 001

Many of us, when we are young, study a language in school, and it may be possible to learn language through this method of an hour three days per week in the classroom (or whatever it may be). However, it is known that the *quickest, most effective* method for learning a new language is through *immersion*. If you move to the country which speaks the language you desire to learn, and you couple living amidst native speakers with active study and practice, you will very quickly learn the language. In a matter of months, if the student is dedicated to practice. We confess, we studied the French language for *three years* in school, and successfully gained *zero ability to speak French.* And that is because, despite the "time" having passed, no energy was input. Because the desire was minimal, the energy was minimal, and nothing was gained. However, when we decided to learn the Greek language, for pleasure, we practiced daily and enjoyed it, and began speaking, reading, and even writing the Greek language in less than two months (with good accent and accuracy). Energy is devoted towards the desired end result: fluency in the Greek language.

Energy and focus will bring what you desire: your opportunity is to practice, and develop the habit of dividing your focused energy on those things that you want to come towards you. When performing mundane tasks, do so on autopilot, and usefully direct your energy thinking about, and imagining what you would like to have coming next. Focus your energy on the desires you wish to see fulfilled. Focus, direct your thoughts during every opportunity. The sweeping and mopping will still happen even if the mind is engaged elsewhere.

Time/energy transmuted to Matter

"Do you mean the principles and theorems of sciences? But these you know are universal intellectual notions, and consequently independent of matter; the denial therefore of this does not imply the denying of them." George Berkeley[84], suggesting "the most extravagant opinion that ever entered the mind of man, to wit, that there is no such thing as "material substance" (matter) in the world."

And, "to exist is one thing, and to be perceived is another." Does matter exist only when it is perceived? That is a question for the philosophers! However, we do possess the power to transmute, through the positive investment of energy, energy into *perceivable* matter. Remember, novice, that what we perceive, everything we experience, exists because the mind comes into play. The "motions and configurations of certain insensible particles of matter," is a fair description of light and color, two things that only exist by the agreement and perception of the mind.

Faith, and it's role in the act of Summoning

"When your faith is tested, your endurance has a chance to grow. So let it grow, for when your endurance is fully developed, you will be strong in character and ready for anything.[85]"

Expand on this thought

"Faith is a state of mind which may be induced, or created, by affirmation or repeated instructions to the subconscious mind (Hill 52)." Re-write and expand this thought before next section.

Faith will develop, on its own accord, so the novice may relax, and rest assured. Through the application and practical test (using the imagination, practicing summoning, et cetera), and the novice will discover, suddenly, that she possess faith, as well, in her tool belt. Remember, even the smallest amount of faith can move mountains (biblical reference). The novice starts with a small seed, which is

---

[84] George Berkeley, Three Dialogues between Hylas and Philonous, 1713.
[85] James 1:3-4 New Living Translation (Tyndale)

perfect, since "the oak tree is contained inside of the acorn." (Source?)

Six steps: revise between the two sets of steps:

1. Idea

2. Mix idea with faith

3. Plan of action is delivered (inspiration)

4. Put plan into action

5. Follow through with plan, using *persistence*

6. Fill your heart and mind with the passionate desire to see your idea become reality

7. Energy is transformed into matter. Idea has become reality. (hill 68)

8. Convince the subconscious mind, by telling yourself repeatedly aloud, that you will receive what you are summoning.

9. You will discover that you, suddenly, have faith that you will receive what you are summoning.

10. Plans for action may be delivered to you, in the form of an inspired thought (follow these thoughts!) that seems to come "out of nowhere."

11. The desired outcome of the summoning will be delivered.

Tested Empirically, 002

As editor of this portion of text, we wish to interject and comment on differing names for the same power, and the power of fluidity of identity, even on the micro-scale. Permit me to illustrate: we have been named, throughout the course of our personal record to this moment, the following names (and corresponding complementary identities): Danielle, nelly, nelly-belly, Nichols-dimes-and-quarters, 'tude, mouth, Dan, Danny, Lady D, D, awesome3, bird, Dee, boto, treal granny, granny, de Medeiros, and also occasionally the standard terms of affection from boyfriends and lovers: babe, baby, honey, et cetera), perhaps most importantly, the family names: Nichols, Howe, de Medeiros,

directly, and many more indirectly. Different identities associated with each stage of development, each stage of social integration, and finally, the present (fluid identity). Your editor is one, though the names are many. Names are one way that people introduce you to some aspect of your character. The name that someone gives you, if it is a "nick-name" is merely their identification of a role that you are living in. your editor has greatly enjoyed being called both "bird," and "granny."

Therefore, remember that there are many names, and, like your editor, the magical energy will respond to any of its names. Call the name that brings you pleasure to call, and your faith requirement will be met.

Ratcheting up belief is a practice that the novice may begin immediately, the instant that she has decided to embrace magical living—and, like the rest of magical living, is easy once she's made the decision to do so. By beginning with small evidences, evidences that that she has the power to believe in, she may, step-by-step, ratchet up to believing in bigger and bigger things. Setbacks may occur, but they serve, often, as wormholes in the time-space continuum between points A and Z (the desire and the fulfillment of desire), so, if the witch experiences a setback, she ought to rejoice and plunge forward with good faith, knowing that any setback results in many steps forward, if she permits it.

Free yourself from the imprisonment of "prejudices derived from common sense, from the habitual beliefs of [your] age or nation, and from convictions which have grown up in [your] mind without *the cooperation and consent of [your] deliberate reason* (Russell, 1912).

It may seem, to the novice, at first glance, to seem contradictory to find the above sentence under the sectional heading "faith." However let me point out, and demonstrate, that most persons, magical or otherwise, take it on *faith* that the sun will rise each day. Never mind that our planet is rotating according to the laws of the universe, and what we perceive as "rising." Does the sun rise? No, the earth rotates around the sun, as it spins on its axis. Nonetheless, we take it on faith that the sun will "rise" in regular, reliable cycles. Reason provides balance in the novice (curious, and adept), and it will benefit the practitioner to embrace reason. Test on faith, and results will give you a reason to continue practice and believe. Test it, find it to be true, and adequately justify belief.

Persistence

Sail to desired shore, burn ships, conquer.

Persistence is the practical reality of faith; if you've got persistence, then you've got faith. Magical living, like any other method of personal living, requires persistent practice if you wish to become adept. The practice of the principles that are our magical heritage is what facilitates delivery between what the desired outcome is, and whether or not you are living in the reality where that outcome has translated to the physical from the purely imaginative—from the source.

The way to succeed in magical living is through persistence, and persistence is easier when you think about it in different lighting—there are many ways to look at it, and the editor will present a few for the novice to consider, and put to practical test. If she permits herself to think like an ancient Greek Commander, then she will set her sights on the shore she desires, sail to that shore, and then burn all the ships. Great commanders did this to illustrate that *success is the only option.* Success or complete annihilation. And of course they succeeded! When faced with annihilation, and given the other option, success, who wouldn't focus on, and actively choose, success?

You will receive what you ask for, although it should be noted that what you ask for might be delivered to you in an unexpected package; practice receiving the small things, and you will be prepared to receive larger things. One step at a time, and persistent practice will make easy the way.

Learn as you go, and edit as you go along. The key thing is to choose to go. It's a delightful journey!

Learning is, of course, an active process. Persistently practice, and you will learn the art of living magically.

Just as each witch may have many names, as was mentioned in the section on faith, the witch has many faces as well. What this means, practically, is that there are many facets, or sides, to her identity and her character. This is true of all persons, whether magical or non-magical, and should come as no surprise to the novice. Since we have many faces, sometimes we will show different faces. This is important, and it comes under the section *"persistence, ´* for an important reason, and it is this: the novice must learn to persistently practice the faces that are in harmony with her desired outcome. If she desires to be a particular thing, whatever that thing may be, she will be that thing as long as she actively practices those faces. A practical application will help to explain further.

Practical application, 001

Whatever path the novice chooses, she must choose *something* if she ever wishes to reach adept status. The good news is that she decides exactly what that is, and it will be the thing that makes her most happy, which is so important to understand that the editor cannot help but continuously repeat it. Regarding faces: have you ever shown your "worst face" to someone? It may occur as a result of impatience, of worry, of fear, or of any of the other negative emotions. And when the novice acts out of those negative feelings and emotions, the face she shows is an unpleasant face. Her best face is what she shows when she is happy, and hopeful, and confident, and loving, and any of the other good feelings. That is the face that she wants people to see and know, and understand as her "true" self. She gets to choose.

The point is that the novice has many faces, as we all do, and if she *persistently practices* wearing the faces that harmonize with her dreams, then her dreams will become reality much sooner. Magic always works, every time, for the good of the novice, if she chooses it. It is important to remember the importance of persistence in this area—until she understands all her faces, and chooses which face to show, she may show faces that she prefers to eradicate. People will see the faces that the witch shows them. Best face forward!

Tested empirically, 001

The editor would like to take a moment, again, to suggest to the reader that the practical advice outline in the handbook is *testable*. While it also embodies a philosophy for a way of living, and behaving (magically), it is, the editor believes, transitioning from philosophy to a science; once a study begins to yield positive, testable results, it has been transmuted from energy to matter. Remember, "the whole study of the heavens, which now belongs to astronoour, was once included in philosophy… thus, to a great extent, the uncertainty of philosophy is *more apparent than real*: those questions which are already capable of definite answers are placed in the sciences, while those only to which, at present, no definite answer can be given, remain to form the residue which is called philosophy (Russell, The Problems of Philosophy, 1912).

Rituals

The rituals are stop-gaps between the good witch and a goddess of destruction. A witch, whether novice or adept, who practices rituals in payment for the delivery of her desires, is a happy, creative creature.

Everything has a price; remember, if you have to ask the price to determine if you can *afford* something, then you cannot afford it. We value that which has a high price—and use this guideline as indicative of value. The beauty of this situation is that you get to decide how you want to pay—the editor recommends that you store up enough gratitude for your biggest dreams and desires, even if those things seem distant from you in the moment. The higher the perceived value of the outcome of our desires, the greater focus of energy required in exchange—learn how to effectively focus your energies, and your every desire will be within reach.

The good things in life are like vampires; their gift is free, and you have to invite them in (at least the first time).

Have courage! The good things come in good company.

Gratitude

Asking for something is same as demanding something, though with a different tone. And this is, for the novice, a valuable nugget of information. When summoning, remember your tone—this is part of demonstrating character. Think of it this way: anyone who has ever managed another person, or persons, may think that the best way to get that person to do what you want is to *tell them what to do.* The editor will affirm, having managed many people over the years, that the most effective, harmonious way to achieve the desired outcome, which is to get someone to do something, is to ask—ask politely, and with sincerity, and trust that your employee will perform the task. The magical flow of energy with which we transform from energy to matter, in the practice of summoning, is much like that employee. Assume that your employee enjoys working for you, loves coming to work, enjoys being productive, and is, in fact, looking for something useful to occupy their time with. The best employee you can imagine. Such an employee works best under gentle guidance, and they may be trusted to complete the job to the specifications you made (it's important to be clear—this employee wants to do it right, let them know your mind!). If you can begin, novice, to think in this way, you will suddenly find that your desired outcome is being fulfilled. Now, keep in mind, this is a stepped process. You asked, you believe that they will perform, you receive the outcome, and

Pay first, then ask. You possess gratitude in abundance; it puts your head in the right place, and you've got an endless supply of it.

you show *gratitude.* It is easiest if you just make the habit of treating that employee, to return to the analogy, always, always, with gratitude. They showed up, you are grateful. They show up every day. They show up every week. And when they are at work, they do what you ask. By showing consistent gratitude for the awesomeness of that employee, that employee will reach even greater heights of awesomeness, creating upward escalating loop of positive energy and reward—reward for the employee in the form of gratitude (and probably, a paycheck), and reward for you in the form of the desired outcome. It begins and ends with understanding how to engage, always, with this state of mind. Make gratitude a garment, and one that you never take off[86].

---

[86] From the section titled, *The Rewards of Wisdom:* "do not let kindness and truth leave

Demonstrating gratitude is one way in which the novice may offer "payment" for the fruits of magical living. Frequently, things will be delivered into the life of the witch through the medium of other people. It is vitally important to recognize the gift, and show gratitude to the universe for delivering the gift, by thanking the messenger of the gift.

The Thank-You note
Is an example of showing gratitude after a gift has been received?

Practicing Hospitality
Demonstrating hospitality is a way of "paying forward" gratitude. A smart witch pays forward far in advance, so that she never finds herself with a debt she cannot pay. Stocking up, or paying forward, is a valuable practice for the witch who lives abundantly.

Hospitality is also one way the Modern Witch demonstrates her mastery over matter: through the culinary arts. Her nose is well trained, and her instincts serve well. She is conversant in cuisine, and she may, at will, sniff out the secrets of another's culinary masterpieces. Reproducing is easy, and she excels particularly in the "free-style" arena. Whether on the range or in the oven, her experiments please. A master of creating something from nothing (a la Button Soup), she confidently delights in entertaining even the trained chef at her dinner parties.

Incantations

There are many ways to utilize incantations, and they a useful method for use when the novice begins mastering the art of Summoning.

An incantation is highly specific, although a rote memorization is useful in the case of the personal mantra (see below), for any specific request. The editor has, therefore, carefully prepared examples and instructions, so that the novice may create their own incantations using the following for educational purposes. Understanding how to effectively use language will greatly assist the novice in her practice, and through practice, the internal and verbal dialogue may be easily

---

you; bind them around your neck, write them on the tablet of your heart, so you will find favor and good repute, in the sight of God and man." –Proverbs 3:3-4 NASB

shifted to create a magical living feedback loop, which is self-sustaining quickly after practice begins.

Instructions:

- Statements must contain only relevant affirmations, since the energy with which we are interacting is positively charged.

What that means is, any negating term is dropped, and only verbs are "heard" by the universe (or gods).

- Sustained focus must be maintained.

Maintain focus, and set up the habit of thinking you are already in possession. It must be summoned, and it is wonderfully useful to summon using the "present tense."

- Practice gratitude.

Payment is required for any transformation of energy or matter, and a smart practitioner is continuously practicing gratitude, and so, in a way, "pays in advance," since she has so much to draw from.

Practical application, 001 (Incantations, 101)

- I will not get sick.

The negation is eliminated, because of the frequency of energy it emits, and therefore instructs your energy, *"I will get sick."* Learn to speak in this way as an alternative:

- I am healthy.

The incantation is accepted in its intended form, and therefore the method of speech to be adopted for promotion of continuous health.

Incantations may be a few words, or of many. What is of vital importance is putting yourself in the spirit of what you are summoning? You must believe what you are saying is true, and you can come to an emotional belief by the intellectual practice of repeating the incantation.

It cannot be repeated enough: incantations must be in the present tense; when words are spoken they become active and alive.

Incantations require belief and commitment (and willingness to pay a price—best to negotiate before any transaction takes place, or you may feel cheated, short-changed, or horrified at the cost negotiated after the fact). They require practice, and the practitioner increases exponentially with practice. The more you use any given incantation, or incantations in general, your efficacy with them increases as well.

[Use our margin notes from T&GR for this section, and notes from Secret—source Secret]]

Mantras

The mantra is a useful tool, and it is your most basic incantation. Use it to summon peace of mind, or to hit the "reset" button on your state of mind. It is specific to the witch who uses it, and it may evolve or change over time. It should be simple, and comforting, and effectively clear away any negative feelings or emotions. It's a powerful tool for the belt of the novice and the adept.

The habit of focused attention:

tested empirically, 001

By developing the habit of focused attention on desired outcomes (which cause good feelings, because they're what you choose and want in life), at first through the incantations, and through the use of the positive emotions (happy imaginings of whatever the novice may desire), eventually those "orders: will override the factory settings, so to speak. The factory settings will provide survival, but only in the most basic sense. The novice "prison breaks" her factory settings, and decides on her own orders. When she does this, and begins living magically, the practices will become more and easier. They will become completely effortless, and that way of thinking and acting will become habit. This is when the novice becomes truly limitless, and graduates herself to adept status. The editor assures the novice, that this is, in fact, quite easy. It

Negative thoughts are the weeds in your garden, and they grow of their own volition, if permitted. Uproot them, and plant, in their place, positive thoughts.

just requires dedicated practice, and the putting to practical test, the practices. They yield results, and build confidence for bigger and better transformations of energy.

Which lead to the active summoning of physical matter (circumstances, experiences, etc.).

(Move incantations up in the text to reflect appropriate order)

Practical application, 001

When a negative thought passes through your mind, as they are wont to do, and then you follow that thought up with *worry* about whether that negative thought (or doubt, or fear, or any other of that motley crew) has ruined all your hard work planting *positive* thoughts—pluck it out! Negative thoughts will come unbidden like mosquitos during rainy season; give them the same attention you'd give a mosquito that enters your home. Notice it, since ignoring it is the same as inviting it to stay, then smash it (or eliminate it in whatever method you prefer), and carry on with whatever you were doing before. Negative thoughts are the weeds in your garden, they show up, but does panicking about them remove them? No. Pull them up, and plant, in their place, positive thoughts.

Negative thoughts can also be thought of like bees or wasps—we have a nice symbiotic relationship with bees, but that's another story; bees and wasps respond to the energy of the person they encounter. It's quite magical, really. If you remain calm, they will either pass you by completely, or, if they've landed on you, leave you in peace. However, if you become terrified, they respond to that terror, and they sting you! And this is unpleasant at best. Both creatures benefit from remaining calm. And just one more analogy using our winged co-inhabitants: negative thoughts can be thought of like flies; they will crawl all over your face and eyes if you get used to them! Shoo them away!

Your mind will take up the suggestion you purposely set before it, or it will take up the suggestions from the ambient environment. This is how magic transmutes energy into matter. The novice need only prime the pump, and once it begins to flow, it will be effortless.

Part Three Recap

- Mastering the Manipulation of energy into matter requires an energy exchange of the following: the novice will be required to "pay" with practice, patience, persistence, belief, understanding, and, most simply, *the desire to do so.*

- We create our reality in our minds first; eject every thought except those thoughts that make you feel good—think upon your desired objective, and think upon all the good things already present in your life.

- Matter comes into existence through the transformation of energy, which takes place in the mind of the witch: it begins in her imagination, then her writing and her speech (her words), and *then*, and only then, does it become "reality."

- "Time" is synonymous with "energy." There is, according to quantum physicist and many great thinkers, no such thing at "time." Think of your life, your thoughts and actions, in terms of energy—how you use your energy, what you use it for, and whether you are happy with the results of what you have spent your energy on. Are you happy with the current results or circumstances? You may begin, immediately, to create pleasant circumstances, by *using your focused energy in exchange for a more desirable reality.*

- Incantations are what we use once we have determined *exactly* what it is that we want, and it's important that we are clear. Anyone who has tried to give a dog five different instructions at once will have a befuddled dog, and the magical flow of energy is the same. Decide exactly what you want: here's a tip. Imagine that you stand before the most powerful person on the planet, and that person has asked you, "What do you want?" The editor recommends that you think as big as you can. Ask for the big, important stuff, and all the other good stuff will come along with it. Incantations are the "orders" we use to train our subconscious mind, which transforms, in the process of summoning, the energy of what we imagine having into the matter of what we possess.

- Belief first in yourself, dear novice, will get you where you wish to go. Believe that you are, indeed, able to decide what you want, and the persistence to acquire whatever it is that may be. Belief will fuel your persistence, and yield results most speedily. Belief can be built, happily, through the use of the incantations. Really, if the novice can first *imagine what she wants,* every other step in the process becomes easy.

- Persistence becomes effortless when it becomes habit. Make the habit of persistently practicing the advice outlined in the handbook, and the novice will have all the tools required

- To elevate herself to adept practitioner—most ideal for the witch, and the world around her.

- Rituals serve a purpose, and are an essential part of the waking life of the novice and adept alike. The ritual of gratitude is *as important* as the rituals of eating or sleeping. The witch may survive some time without any of the three, but she thrive and be happiest when she practices the tone of gratitude. Honor the rituals.

Quick Answer:

Build a wall of immunity against negative influences.

Immunity!

Part Five: Sustaining Magic

Conquering forces of evil

(Placement—before or after origin story?)
"The first and best victory is to conquer self.[87]"

The novice may have been told, or heard, that "love[88] of money is the root of all evil (cite)," however, the helpful editor wishes to shed new light on such a statement, but immediately calling out the *true root of all evil*. Which is, at its most essential, "susceptibility to negative influences.[89]" And susceptibility to negative influences can be helpfully wrapped up under the heading *"fear"*. Fear may go under many different names, yet it remains, *fear*. Fear divides, it separates and isolates, which automatically begins to destroy positive energy. It disrupts the mind with worries and cares, if the witch permits it to. All evil can be traced back, to the careful genealogist, to fear. Let's take a look at fear and its offspring, and what the novice may do to eradicate it from her mind and her life.

(May to update language here—do we use "fear" or "forces of evil," or "root of evil," or just "evil?")

The witch has, at her disposal, all of the tools which will easily and speedily conquer the forces of evil—even the most insidious ones; which is good news, because these are also the most dangerous ones. It has been mentioned throughout the text, but it bears repeating: all of the forces, whether positive or negative, exist as a state of mind. (In the index, list all of the major topics, and the pages that they're referenced—such as "state of mind, see, p. --, etc.")

It is both practical and useful for the witch to master the art of conquering the forces of evil, since if any are present within her mind, she inhibits her ability to summon, and to control the magical flow of energy—and paralyzes magical living. Here, the novice may speedily

---

[87] Plato, citation

[88] Love, by definition, is good. If we experience *love*, in any of its forms, we can be assured that what we are loving is positive, by its very nature being "lovable." Now, it may be true that some practitioners mix up their priorities, and cause harm to themselves or to loved ones, but this is a fault in the mind of the person causing the harm. Responsibility must be laid where it is due.

[89] Hill 358

learn what she may use to face and conquer the forces of evil in any form.

When the novice can confidently, fearlessly, and courageously look straight at [whatever frightens her], then she has truly conquered the forces of evil—indecision, doubt, and fear[90]. Let's get busy with conquering them.

The forces of evil are far less obvious than the novice may think, and that is due to the insidious nature of such—they work by sneaking in when we are off-guard, and, like a big spider to the arachnephobic, they may be allowed to reside because the novice fears directly confronting them and issuing them their marching orders, "out!" The novice has great power. The power of the novice is equal to that of the adept, and the difference between the two statuses is, quite simply, that the adept witch is in the habit of continuous practice of the principles that are illustrated in the advice of the handbook. And one other trait separates novice and adept: the adept is still harassed by fears, but does she let them in? No. she looks, with great clarity and purpose, inside her own mind, as habit, to clear it out of any fears or other negative influences.

We are always drawing to us energy that harmonizes with our thoughts.

Make the habit of fixing your thoughts.

A child thinks that if they cannot see something, that thing goes away—hiding under the covers to escape boogey men, or covering the eyes with the hands during the scary parts of a movie. The novice may make the mistake of doing this, when she first begins practice, and that is why this section on conquering the forces of evil is relegated to the final chapter, instead of the first. The novice may think that by ignoring her fears, they will cease to exist, and for some powerful witches, that might be true. But for the rest of us, let us take a stern, unflinching look, at the start of each day, and make sure our minds are clear and free, and *completely under our own control.* We have but one thing in our waking life that we may control completely,

---

[90] Hill 324

and that is our own mind. Uninvited guests might buzz in, like a fly when the screen-door is open; why burn down the house or call the police when a fly buzzes in? We notice it, and then we remove it, or we kill it. Such it is with the forces of evil. Examine your mind, each time you rise from sleep, and periodically, throughout the waking day. By training the sub-conscious mind (through the practices outlined earlier), the witch alleviates herself of the burden of having to actively, consciously, perform this task. The short cut, to know if she's mastered this skill, is to simply go about her day, and trust her feelings to warn her if her thoughts have been derailed. They are easily set aright by the witch who understands and practices thought-impulse control. The forces of evil are *states of mind*.

Let's take a closer look.

Tested with Reason, 001

Good energy and bad energy can be thought of as masks that we put on. Bad energy is the mask that attaches itself to your face, rudely, without having been placed there by the witch. Simply remove the mask! By using the *mirror*, as was advised under "home décor" the witch can check her face. She will quickly learn to differentiate, by looking in the mirror, what mask she is wearing. Fearlessly look into the mirror, as it is a wonderfully useful tool for this purpose. Have courage, look, and really *see*. This will prove helpful, especially once it has become a check-point in the daily life. Likewise, all of the "good masks" are easily visible to the witch in the mirror, however, these are fine masks, and must be picked up by the witch, and worn with purpose. If you are feeling bad for any reason at all, fix your face.

We defeat them swiftly, by knowing exactly what we want, belief that we will succeed, and acting with courage to persist; and once we have made a habitual practice of doing these three things, we are in the position to enjoy what we receive—which will be our desired outcome. Has something wandered in the open door of your daydreams? Shut the door tight! Make your daydreams, and your mind, and your life, "invitation only." (Might rewrite for clarity)

Open the door to all who knock, but only invite in what is good. You may engage with any and all on the patio, and do so with grace and magic. Carefully examine your thinking, and ask yourself hard questions—are you permitting any fear, doubt, or indecision to reside there? Settle the mind with these practical incantations which will assist the novice:

- Our thoughts are *invitation only.*

- I am immune[91] to indecision, doubt, and fear.

- I am awake and aware.

Practically, it is good to understands that the forces of evil are insidious—they are those rude party-crashers that enter without invitation. The gracious hostess doesn't make a fuss, *however*--only that which she invites in may stay. Her mind, as well as her parties, are "invitation only." Uninvited guests will attempt to enter both, and how the witch deals with these will determine her character. You can tell something of the character of a person, whether witch, or daughter of Eve, by how they treat those who can *do nothing for them.* Whether it is a person, or a force, behave always with grace. If we have learned anything through ourthology, it is that sometimes an angel, or a prince, or a powerful entity, will masquerade as something else. The adept witch is gracious to all, and draws her boundaries firmly and gently.

She will always be gracious to the uninvited who crash her parties, but she will eradicate the uninvited from her mind.

(Transition)

Tested with Reason, 001

The snake comes to the woman in the garden, and facilitates the turning on of lights, so to speak. At least, the woman blames the snake for her actions, when she wakes up (and the editor suggests that this woman is Lilith, who is, later in the chapter of Genesis, replaced with Eve) and is questioned about how she came to know the secret of the knowledge of good and evil (eating from the tree of wisdom).

The less *visible* the thing, the more control we have over it.

The adept witch has absolute control over her thoughts.

---

[91] Immunity really helps the witch to relax and enjoy herself.

The snake's punishment? That woman will fear the bite of the snake, and if she fears the snake, how will the snake get close enough to turn on the lights for her? Alternately, the snake will fear being crushed by the heel of the woman, and may avoid getting close enough to permit her liberation. The editor recommends, *eat apples, and charm snakes!*

Temporary setbacks may occur, in this, as in anything else that the novice is practicing. There may, still, be moments of sheer terror—the witch handles great power, and with that great power comes responsibility. The desired outcomes of each witch will be different, and the tests of each witch will likewise, be different. Nonetheless, whatever the witch chooses, she may rest assured—she will only be given those tests she has the capacity to pass. Sometimes lessons are repeated, but this happens, mostly, because the witch either hasn't yet wakened to her powers, or hasn't realized that a test is being administered. Sometimes the test is, as they say in the research community, "blind," or even, "double-blind," if the lesson comes through a third party (a person in the life of the novice). Take heart! A solution to every test will always be available to the witch, and it will be an easy and pleasant solution—*this is how she will know it is the correct solution.*

Best face forward! The adept witch practices facing *everything and anything* fearlessly, courageously, and with grace.

"Indecision crystalizes into doubt; the two blend and become fear![92]"

Simply be firm and clear about the things that you really want, and the novice may effectively wipe out all doubt and fear! It is, truly, this simple a solution.

"What do you really, truly, want?" Decide. Once you decide what you want, you will be able to see an easy solution to getting what you want[93]. Payment will be required, but that payment will be a pleasant exchange. Take courage in this truth, and you too, novice,

---

[92] Hill 324

[93] It may be relevant to mention that this occured *before* the publication of the handbook, it occurred *before* the book was sold to a publisher, and the editor was acting on a pure exchange of energy (put to use through desire, belief, and persistence), for matter (product for the editor, spokesperson for the brand)

will easily conquer fear, doubt, and all their other scrawny gang of pals.

"Conquer self and force Life to pay whatever is asked.[94]"

Perfection

"... but perfect yourself first."[95]

Mastery is delivered when the practices are put to useful test, and when those practices become *habit*. The novice graduates to adept when she begins to practice through the habitual testing and use of *all of the practices*. The practices have been delivered, and reiterated, in many ways throughout the handbook. The editor has also made use of Practical Tests, and Practical Applications, to aid and assist the novice in easing the transition into magical living. When the transition occurs, dear novice, it will be a breath of relief and fresh air. For your edification and benefit, the editor has provided a few thoughts on Perfection, which is the last chapter in the modern witch's handbook.

Practice makes perfect, and perfect practice of living magically is its own reward.

Perfection, from the outside (from a third party viewer), looks effortless. This is because it is practiced to perfection. Think of the most famous ballet dancers, or the most proficient violinists; to watch them practice or demonstrate their "work," it appears to come to them effortlessly.

Vivacious and gracious, the modern witch is memorable.

And it appears effortless because it is perfect. Perfection comes only to those who practice, and, with practice comes suffering (depending on the particular lesson). The good news is that suffering causes a lesson to be taught deeply, and effectively, and such lessons learned stick with the novice, even though life-cycles.

"Remember too, that all who succeed in life get off to a bad start, and pass through many heartbreaking struggles before they "arrive" (Hill 33-34)."

---

[94] Hill 373
[95] Carnegie, 26

Perfection is, once achieved, continuously maintained through energetic rehearsal and practice. The violinist does continuously picks up his bow even after he masters his instrument, and the ballerina continues to wear out practice shoes when she's the prima. That moment of having achieved perfection, it could be argued, is just the beginning of their careers.

The Adept is the one who practices without ceasing, and perfection is balanced, adept, practice

A natural born witch is blessed, in that she naturally possess many gifts. When such gifts "come naturally," she is able to practice multiple disciplines, disparate though they may seem, effectively and with what approaches perfection. Should she focus her attention on her natural talents, rather than continuously sampling, she will achieve perfection at an accelerated rate, and maintain said perfection for so long as she desires to do so.

Remember, you have the power to write your own story. When you begin to actively, wakefully practice the art of writing your own story, you will have graduated from novice to adept.

True balance is as close to perfection as any living creature can hope to attain. Learn to practice without cease, without neglecting the things that are important in your life. It's called balance, because it requires some focused attention; but when you know that you must do it, you will discover that it is quite easy.

An exciting side-effect of magical living, when practiced perfectly, is the complete freedom from competition and jealousy; this freedom arrives in golden shoes, when the novice begins to occupy her waking life with only those projects and labors which she produces. Things she truly believes in, whether she is the source of the project, or an invited member to the project team or practice.

But the real truth of it is, if the practitioner can handle it, is that she will have to get a little bit broken, but just enough to let out the good bits. The magic flows out of those broken bits, so submit to the lessons of life, and remember that on the other end is a truly beautiful, and magical life. *"The fleetest beast to bear you to perfection is suffering."*[96]

Tested with Reason, 001

The editor takes a moment to mention a few helpful tips for the novice[97] alongside all of the advice offered by the cumulative history of hundreds of lifetimes of witches represented in that heritage shared by all natural born witches and shared with you here in *The Modern Witch*, and it is this: there is a net in which you may easily carry all of the lessons you have found worth placing in your own magical living tool-belt—conquer fear of losing or forgetting your new tools as you walk through life, whether you choose the dirt road or the tractor beam, and that net is responsibility. If you are willing to take responsibility for your thoughts, then anything else that comes your way you will glide through effortlessly and easily. Denying responsibility is equal to self-immolation, whether you set yourself on fire in a public square, or live inside a life that brings you dread, fear, worry, or other unhappiness.

You may be wondering, novice witch, what we chose. We choose *wisdom*. Knowing how to do the right thing at the right time goes a long way towards all other portals to happiness.

Now, remember, what is *perfect* for each witch may vary. The editor provides this information because it has been useful for her, and it may help to shed light for the novice on the larger ideas which will help her live *her* perfectly magical life.

For the editor, Wisdom is, among other things, and quite practically, knowing *what* to summon, once you understand the power at your fingertips.

Lessons from the magical in history, 001 (or whatever it's called)

⁵ In Gibeon the LORD appeared to Solomon in a dream at night; and God said, "Ask what *you wish* Me to give you."
Solomon's Prayer

---

[96] Master Eckhardt
[97] Each tip offered with sincerity by the editor are suggestions meant to speed the novice witch along towards adept practice.

⁶ Then Solomon said, "You have shown great loving-kindness to Your servant David our father, according as he walked before You in ⁽ᵃ⁾truth and righteousness and uprightness of heart toward You; and You have ⁽ᵇ⁾reserved for him this great loving-kindness, that You have given him a son to sit on his throne, as it is this day. ⁷ Now, O LORD our God, You have made Your servant king in place of our father David, yet I am but a little child; I do not know how to go out or come in. ⁸ Your servant is in the midst of Your people which You have chosen, a great people who are too many to be numbered or counted. ⁹ So give Your servant ⁽ᶜ⁾an understanding heart to judge Your people to discern between good and evil. For who is able to judge this ⁽ᵈ⁾great people of Yours?⁹⁸ "

"Wisdom is a tree of life to those who embrace her; happy are those who hold her tightly.⁹⁹"

We may, as magically inclined, re-enter the Garden of Eden, and eat from the tree of life; embrace wisdom, and experience life the way you were meant to.

It's interesting to note, here, that the King Solomon asked for the same gift that *the woman* took, for herself and shared with Adam, in Genesis, with vastly different results. Perhaps because Solomon asked for the gift when a gift was offered, while the woman took what she wanted without asking?

"The woman¹⁰⁰ was convinced. The fruit looked so fresh and delicious, and it would make her so wise! So she ate some of the fruit. She also gave some to her husband, who was with

---

⁹⁸ 1 Kings 3:5-9. New American Standard Bible (NASB)

⁹⁹ Proverbs 3:18 New Living Translation

¹⁰⁰ Adam doesn't name his wife until after this episode. He doesn't claim a wife until after the tree eating—it is possible that the woman who gave him the fruit was, indeed, Lilith, his first wife—the one Adam calls, "the woman You gave me" (who brought him the fruit, when questioned by god.)

Lilith is the ancestress of all witches, (make note and expand this thought in the appendix), while it is Eve who becomes "the mother of all people everywhere."

her. Then he ate it, too. At that moment, their eyes were opened...[101] "

The editor can't say whether is relevant or important, and mentions it only to stir the curiosity (of which the novice is blessed with in great capacity) of the novice, and give her freedom to decide for herself if there is any meaning to it.

It is recommended, by the editor, that the novice ask for everything and anything she desires. Ask, and it will be yours. The editor also recommends that the novice ask before taking anything, and refrain from taking anything unless it has been asked for or offered (use caution in what you ask for, novice! Ask for all the good stuff!).

Note on the word "wisdom" comes from, in the usage adopted by the editor, the Hebrew text in 1 Kings; the word is translated as "Chokhmah" (khok-ma), and means, wisdom for practical living, and is a high level of wisdom.

For us, wisdom is the perpetual spring from which flows *all of the other things we wish to possess.*

Tested with Reason, 001

What the novice chooses, and selects as her primary desired objective, will determine (if we may borrow from the example demonstrated by the cloisters within the Catholic church) the "order" that she has committed herself to, and the "orders" that she receives (and applies through the outlet of her talents) will be relevant to the "order" that she has aligned herself to. As practical example, the Benedictine order of nuns has different rules than the Franciscan order of nuns; they peacefully coexist, and when traveling, nuns may stay within the cloister or at the convent of other orders (and happily), when they are at home, practicing their orders, they practice the orders specific to their Order. It can also be thought of like a pirate ship: each captain has his own rules, and they may be different on each ship, but the ship still sails on the oceans (or other body of water) and it still employs a first mate, and deck hands, and so on. Regardless of who the captain, or the mother superior is, each has its own way of doing things. Such is the choice of the novice witch and per primary desired outcome.

---

[101] Genesis 3:6-7, NLT

The editor confidently believes that the novice, if she follows her heart, will choose exactly what is perfect *for her.*

principles for practicing perfection

With everything that has been said, let's take a moment and review what have been major themes throughout the handbook.

1. The habit of continuous practice. Keeping on keeping on, going above and beyond the minimum requirements. This practice will yield the fastest, most abundant results, and it comes from doing and being your best at everything you do. Apply magic at all times, to every action, and every action will become magical. See how quickly you arrive in your desired outcome once you begin this!

2. Clarity of vision, or the clear definition of your desired outcome. When you finally define exactly what it is that you want, and you focus your full attention on that thing, then you will begin to rapidly draw that thing towards you. When thoughts of this outcome pervade your every waking moment, and you've trained your mind to subconsciously dwell upon your desires, then you are in excellent position to see those desires fulfilled. Will the delivery person from the Chinese restaurant show up at your house with the full menu? Well, by golly, he will if you order it. You will get exactly what you order, once you have decided what you want, and made clear your order.

3. Harmonious pairings and partnerships. When two or more can agree about something, then that thing will begin to happen. The key point is that you find someone, or several persons, who have dreams that overlap with yours; in this way, you can harness the power of your collected magic, and amplify it. Highly recommended for the novice with big dreams.

4. Mastering the mental state through the active direction of the emotions. Consciously replacing all negative thoughts and feelings with positive, affirmative thoughts and feelings that are in harmony with your desired outcome.

5. Being yourself, better. By practicing and applying the principles of magical living, the novice will become better and better at each of those aspects, and in essence, become the best version of herself. Her idealized self. This is the self that can achieve any heights that the novice may imagine.

6. The ability to see every situation as an opportunity for learning, and therefore positive and working harmoniously towards the desired outcome, or created reality. Regardless of past circumstances, or the perception of defeat, if you begin to train your mind to accept each instance as a benefit to you, as an learning experience under your belt—*they will become so.* Every defeat or temporary setback is a training ground, and embracing and accepting the lesson will accelerate the novice quickly towards adept status.

7. Embrace all of the senses, including the sixth. Learn to trust your gut, and to trust your instincts, and they will serve you well. This is the place where you may, if you choose, touch genius.

8. Understanding that you *have the power* to control your reality, and actively taking control of that reality. Understanding that what you believe is more important than what appears to be true, especially when you begin to practice magic (before evidences of success have begun to pile up). And pushing forward regardless of what the circumstances may appear to be.

9. Learn to balance your power with your mind through the practice of discipline: listening to your body, developing the habit of continuous practice in all areas. Uplifting your thinking with continuous education of the mind, whether that education is from a school, a person, a book, or nature, fill your mind with those explorations that enliven it, as habitual practice.

10. Focus. While your character will automatically begin to improve the moment you begin practice (it is inevitable), and your life will begin to improve overall, if there is a specific desired outcome you wish to see fulfilled, such as the fulfillment of particular hopes and dreams, or financial success, then you will require focus. Focus may be achieved through the building of habit through discipline, and that which you focus on will be drawn into your life, through the law of summoning.

11. State of mind. State of mind is infectious, and whatever your state of mind is will spread, provided that your mind is stronger than the minds that are around you. A strong, healthy, focused mind will secure the cooperation of others, thus further uplifting your efforts, whatever they may be. Remember, while you may get much done on your own, novice, while practicing the principles contained within the handbook, if you wish to achieve great heights, you will, at one time or another, require the cooperation of others—best to have the willing, enthusiastic cooperation!

12. The highest law. The highest law in magic is the highest law in any other realm, and simply put, it is love. While there are many varieties and ways in which we love, it is the practical kind of loving that is the daily practice of the novice and adept alike. It amounts

to the Golden Rule: do unto others as you would have them do unto you. This is essential, and if you practice no other principle in the handbook, it is recommended that you learn to practice this law speedily. This is the law that will secure you in the affections of those around you, which will uplift you faster than any other of the principles when practiced with focus. This small endeavor will immediately begin to change your life, and is quite easy to put into practice: simply believe, for your own purposes, that every action you perform is witnessed by an observer. In this way, you can be sure that your motives are always in sync with your desired outcome, and you will be blameless before any observer.

Re-cap of all the major points from the text (fill in after they're flushed out in the main body, might to move to a different area in the book—after appendix?)

Introduction recap

Desire to practice is the most important element, and is available to all. The novice who practices is the happiest witch.

Part One

Magicality in daily life

Planning

Occupation of energies

Energetic exchanges

Education and increase in talents

Part Two

- The seat of emotions
- Relationships
- The mind

Part Three

- Mastering the Manipulation of energy into matter requires an energy exchange of the following: the novice will be required to "pay" with practice, patience, persistence, belief, understanding, and, most simply, *the desire to do so.*

- We create our reality in our minds first; eject every thought except those thoughts that make you feel good—think upon your desired objective, and think upon all the good things already present in your life.

- Matter comes into existence through the transformation of energy, which takes place in the mind of the witch: it begins in her imagination, then her writing and her speech (her words), and *then*, and only then, does it become "reality."

- "Time" is synonymous with "energy." There is, according to quantum physicist and many great thinkers, no such thing at "time." Think of your life, your thoughts and actions, in terms of energy—how you use your energy, what you use it for, and whether you are happy with the results of what you have spent your energy on. Are you happy with the current results or circumstances? You may begin, immediately, to create pleasant circumstances, by *using your focused energy in exchange for a more desirable reality.*

- Incantations are what we use once we have determined *exactly* what it is that we want, and it's important that we are clear. Anyone who has tried to give a dog five different instructions at once will have a befuddled dog, and the magical flow of energy is the same. Decide exactly what you want: here's a tip. Imagine that you stand before the most powerful person on the planet, and that person has asked you, "What do you want?" The editor recommends that you think as big as you can. Ask for the big, important stuff, and all the other good stuff will come along with it. Incantations are the "orders" we use to train our subconscious mind, which transforms, in the process of summoning, the energy of what we imagine having into the matter of what we possess.

- Belief first in yourself, dear novice, will get you where you wish to go. Believe that you are, indeed, able to decide what you want, and the persistence to acquire whatever it is that may be. Belief will fuel your persistence, and yield results most speedily. Belief can be built, happily, through the use of the incantations. Really, if the novice can first *imagine what she wants,* every other step in the process becomes easy.

- Persistence becomes effortless when it becomes habit. Make the habit of persistently practicing the advice outlined in the handbook, and the novice will have all the tools required

- To elevate herself to adept practitioner—most ideal for the witch, and the world around her.

- Rituals serve a purpose, and are an essential part of the waking life of the novice and adept alike. The ritual of gratitude is *as important* as the rituals of eating or sleeping. The witch may survive some time without any of the three, but she thrive and be happiest when she practices the tone of gratitude. Honor the rituals.

- Lessons from the Appendix

Put magic to the test; it delivers *every time.*
May you be favored by all gods.

Danielle de Medeiros, May 2, 2013

Appendix

The Witches, an Origin Tale

At the beginning of time, when the earth was new, and all creation fresh sprung from the imagination of the gods, there were creatures divided into four ranks: first the gods, then the angels, then mankind, then animals. The gods ruled all the creatures, and each rank of creatures ruled the creatures below themselves.

The gods created the earth, and all the things in the earth, and gave animals of like kind one to another, commanding them to multiply and fill up the earth. The gods also gave mankind, male and female, to each other, commanding them also to multiply. Among the race of men, there were two lineages: the daughters of Eve, called the daughters of god, and the daughters of Lilith, called daughters of men.

But to the angels, where was their kind? For the angels were made male, and females of their kind were not found. These angels entertained themselves by watching the earth, and made themselves princes of the earth.

During this time, there lived a man named Mntoch, much loved by the gods. There was no one on earth more favored among men. Mntoch lived 461 years in abundance, then dwelt with the gods.

After some time, as the earth became filled up with men and animals, the angels looked around the earth, and said one to another, "all of creation has been given the command, "multiply and fill up the earth," but to us, the gods have given no females." So the angels again looked around the earth, and they saw that the daughters of men were beautiful; so beautiful, in fact, that once the angels looked upon them, they could not look away, but burned with desire to possess them for their own. It came to pass that the angels took to wife the daughters of men, and fathered a race of children upon them.

The angels taught their wives, and also their daughters, things unknown to the daughters of god: oursterious arts, bewitching music, and the secrets of cosmetics. Because of this knowledge, the wives of angels surpassed all other women, and became the Sirens of old, desired above all women. Children born of Sirens and angels are of two variety: first, they bore the heroes of renown, giants among men, handsome and brave warriors. They entered no battle that they did not win. Terrifying adversaries they were, feared by men and loved by the daughters of men and the daughters of god. These sons became so great that they surpassed men in all things—including wickedness. The daughters of god were turned from right ways because of their love for the Heroes, forgetting their virtue. Sons were born that did not resemble husbands, and men cried out saying, "the Heroes have seduced our wives!"

Also born of the union between the daughters of men and angels were the Witches. Women who possessed the beauty of their mothers, the skills and talents taught their mothers, and, unlike their brothers the Heroes, the Witches were gifted with magicality and the *option* of immortality.

When the angels looked around the earth, they saw their wives, the Heroes, their sons, and the Witches, their daughters. Seeing all the havoc that their families had wrought on the sons and daughters of god, the angels said to one another, "if the gods look upon the earth, and see what we have done, surely they will punish us, since our wives, daughters and sons have all the good things of the earth for themselves, leaving the sons of god only a little better off than the animals." They were afraid.

And so, the angels called Mntoch, beloved of the gods, saying to him, "Go to the gods on our behalf, and tell them what we have done. Intercede for us, so that they will not be angry with us and punish us, or destroy us or our families for this thing we have done."

So Mntoch went before the gods, saying, "The angels have taken as wives the daughters of men, teaching them dark secrets not known to men. Their sons are giants in the land, consuming that which they have not sown, and their daughters are magical, casting spells on the sons and daughters of god."

The gods were angered at this news, and looked upon the earth saying, "Destroy it all, and begin again, for our creation has been ruined by this thing that the angels and their offspring have done."

But Mntoch answered the gods, interceding on the angels' behalf, saying, and "surely there is another way?"

Because of the love born Mntoch by the gods, they considered his plea, then rendered judgment, saying, "Let the Sirens become barren, so that the sons will not be born to them again. The Heroes, because of their wickedness, shall die, and their spirits roam the earth until the end of time. Let them pester wicked men so they will know how the gods view wickedness. Let the Witches live, but let them be feared by the sons and daughters of god. And let the angels watch, that they may see all the trouble they have caused."

This is the origin of the Witches.

**

●●

Note for re-write of critical analysis:

Remind the reader that the Nephilim were the offspring of both angels and human women—while angels are technically "non-gendered," (we typically attribute masculine sex to them), human women donate an x- chromosome, so it holds that her offspring would also have at least one x- chromosome—we know of the Nephilim, and the argument holds that there were also female offspring of the women and watchers, and, perhaps we never heard of them because *they were women,* and that period in history was patriarchal, and the females were mostly ignored. So, the female offspring of the mortal/divine pairing could carry the gifts of "the angels" in their bloodline. And we could call such offspring, and therefore descendants, witches—if we liked.

Witches are, as it happens, the sole offspring of angels (Watchers) remaining on this planet, since their blood brothers, the Nephilim, were destroyed in the flood, and the few that remain have gone insane and live like animals in the remotest forests of the earth, where they have for thousands of years. The benevolence of the vast majority of witches should assure the curious non-magical of the benign and helpful nature of both the witches, and the watchers, who sired them. (The Nephilim were bonkers because the human X chromosome didn't play well with the androgynous Watcher chromosome.)

You're just too good to be true: angels "Fall" for mortal women: a careful look at source materials.

"Can't take our eyes off of you. You'd be like heaven to touch

*I wanna hold you so much, at
long last love has arrived, and I
thank god I'm alive. You're just
too good to be true, can't take our
eyes off of you."*[102]

Angels in love with women, forsaking the unlimited glories of heaven *and,* possibly their very divinity[103] for a night of passion… the kind of epic romance the Four Seasons barely scratched the surface of. But it's a bible story I'm thinking of, a story millennia old. When examining the Genesis text, our attention was immediately captivated by the pericope in chapter six: the *sole* mention of the Watchers—the angels charged with watching over the earth, and while on duty, fell in love with mortal women, a pairing which produced, what the author of Genesis calls, *Nephilim.* This particular story appears as the introduction to a much larger narrative: that of the Great Flood. The inclusion and placement of this mention of Nephilim seems to suggest that the actions of the Watchers (and their offspring) were responsible (at least partly) for the apocalypse that follows—a great flood wipes out all the life on earth, and with that destruction of life, also wipes out the wickedness taking place within it.

Who were the Nephilim? Why did the author mention them at all? If we know anything about the construction of the biblical cannon, is that it has survived trimming for thousands of years, when we're talking about the Pentateuch all the way up through the Pseudoepigrapha. And that only the most essential details survived—or the most perfect, or… whatever measure was used, we can rest assured, they did allow anything to remain that was *not* essential to the narrative. So what part did this narrative play in God's decision to destroy the world with a flood? If, indeed, heavenly beings and their half-mortal offspring were the root cause of the apocalypse, then certainly their story deserves more than a single paragraph in Genesis? Instead, while the genesis account alludes to the Nephilim, the blame for the annihilation of all but one family is accorded to humans themselves—perhaps for allowing the Nephilim to do what they did? For being seduced by the angels in the first place? For worshipping the heroes that resulted from those unions? Let's get some more information.

---

[102] Lyrics by Bob Crewe and Bob Gaudio
[103] You don't know what you don't know.

The antediluvian account in genesis tells us very little. We learn that the Nephilim are giants: the offspring of the Sons of Gods (or Watchers) and the daughters of men. Which leads to the question: Who were the sons of God? There are several theories, our two favorites (which also happen to be the more popular theories among people who care) are, on one hand thrilling, and on the other, logical. We do so love both logic and thrills. They are, first: the Sons of God are actual angels who come down to the earth to take the daughters of men (human mortal women) as wives (Bautch 766), and second: the sons of god are the descendants of Adam and Eve's son Seth (who keep to "true" religion), while the daughters of men are the female descendants of Cain (pagans) ("City of God").

Early Christians adopted the first theory (at least, for a few hundred years), that the sons of god are in fact fallen angels that had intimate relations with mortal women, so it's from this perspective we offer analysis. But first, let's take a brief look at the history of the story of the Watchers.

In the book of Genesis, we read, "Enoch walked with God; and he was not, for God took him" (Genesis 5:24, RSV). Later chapters in the books attributed to Enoch are apocalyptic in nature, and having the status of being the only human being (besides the prophet Elijah) to ascend directly into the Divine presence in heaven makes Enoch uniquely qualified to be familiar with heaven's secrets (Harris 305).

Jewish books written between 200 BCE and 200 CE fall into two broad categories: the Apocrypha, and the Pseudoepigrapha (Harris 305). These books, written in Hebrew, Aramaic, and Greek, include "wisdom literature, history, short stories, and apocalyptic literature" ("Apocrypha and Pseudoepigrapha"). While some books were read and considered credible by Jews during that period, none of the books became part of the cannon of Jewish, or later Christian, scriptures. The book of Enoch, which may be the oldest surviving apocalyptic book (Harris 305), is a collection of texts by many unknown authors composed over a period of up to 300 years (Nickelsburg vii). The authorship is attributed to the antediluvian patriarch from the book of Genesis; the use of a pseudonym in this type of literature was not uncommon during the period, nor does the practice seem to have been frowned upon or considered inherently unreliable (Harris 305).

The tale of the Watchers, and the book of Enoch as a while, were popular with early Christians (and referenced in the standard New

Testament cannon as authoritative), influencing some great theologians of the time, and were defended by the noted apologist Tertullian among others (Kvanvig). Even at the height of popularity, the Enochian texts were not accepted by all the churches, and after the denunciation in Augustine's "City of God," they became disused and eventually forgotten in all but the orthodox Ethiopian church. Because the Ethiopian church was geographically isolated from the rest of the church, the books of Enoch (1 & 2) were retained as authoritative, and continued to be copied along with the other texts in the cannon. It wasn't until the 18th century that a translation of the texts was found in Abyssinia, and before the fragments discovered with the Dead Sea Scrolls at Qumran in 1952, no Aramaic copies of the text were extant (Harris 305). We can thank the Ethiopic church, since, it were not for their scholarly diligence, and it is likely that no complete copies of the book of Enoch would have survived antiquity.

The exact date of the writing of the story of the Watchers is unknown, but it is possible that it was as early as 300 BCE (Kvanvig 167). It is, however, accepted that the "oldest Enochic writings...existed in the period when the Hebrew Bible was formed" (Kvanvig 167). This helps to explain why the texts would have been so familiar to New Testament authors such as Jude (Jude 1:14, quoting Enoch 1:9).

The story of the Watchers is found in Genesis, as we already know, and in greater detail in the book attributed to Enoch, in a section consisting of 36 chapters, called simply, "The book of the Watchers" (Harris 305). It is to this book we will turn to find a more complete telling of the story introduced to us in Genesis.

In genesis, we find the account of the Watchers:

"when men began to multiply on the face of the ground, and daughters of men were born to them, the sons of god saw that the daughters of men were fair; and they took to wife such of them as they chose" (Genesis 6:1-2 RSV).

It serves only to pique interest...

Compare to the Enoch 1 account:

"When the sons of men had multiplied, in those days, beautiful and comely daughters were born to them. And the watchers, the sons of heaven, saw them and desired them. And they said to one another, "Come, let us choose for ourselves wives from the daughters of men, and let us beget children for ourselves" (1 Enoch 6:1-2).

While each accounting begins nearly identically, and both texts agree that the daughters of men were "women... so beautiful that even the angels in heaven could not resist them" (Kvanvig), upon further reading we discover that the Enochian account is both far more detailed, and offers more in the way of explain its reason for placement in genesis preceding the account of the flood. One wonders if the story of the watchers, as recalled in 1 Enoch, was general (or folk) knowledge among its early audience. Such supposition may serve to explain the brevity of the account in genesis.

The book 1 Enoch is divided into five sections: the first, the Book of the Watchers (1 Enoch 1-36) being pertinent to our interest. It is from this text we discover that it was "rebel angels that introduced evil into the world" (Nickelsburg 1) and sinful humans guilty of perpetuating that evil, against whom god renders his wet judgment.

The sin of the watchers were many: not only did they covet the daughters of men as wives, and sire monstrous offspring (reaching up to 1500 meters in height) on them, they also instructed humans in arts heretofore forbidden mankind: magic, warfare, jewelry, and cosmetics: the latter causing women to become even more dangerously irresistible to men (Kvanvig 164). The Nephilim, those horrendous offspring of the Watchers and the daughters of men, committed crimes arguable worse than those of their fathers: making humans' food-producing slaves, and, when the food ran out, eating the humans instead; later, even eating each other (Kvanvig 164). It was this series of events that caused humans to call on heaven for relief... "Their groan has come up to the gates of heaven, and it does not cease..." (1 Enoch 9:10). Although god, in this account, answered humanity's cry from earth, and intervened with the flood "destroy[ing] all perversity from the face of the earth," interestingly, only Noah and his immediate family were deemed worthy to populate the new post-deluvian earth (1 Enoch 10:16).

We find this bit strange—if it was the humans, not just Noah, crying out for relief from the atrocities inflicted upon them by the divine beings, why wipe out all of humanity? Why not just the perpetrators of wickedness?

After the flood event, Enoch is sent from Heaven, where he had been "blessing the Lord," with a message for the Watchers, informing them that because of their actions, they "will have no peace or forgiveness" (1 Enoch 12:5). Enoch then obediently goes and shares this message with the Watchers, who are "...all afraid, and trembling and fear seized them" (1 Enoch 13:3). The response of the Watchers, after hearing these ill tidings from Enoch, is to request that Enoch intercede on their behalf, and present a petition to god. They request, through Enoch, that they might be forgiven their crimes, since they themselves are too ashamed to ask god for themselves (1 Enoch 13:4). After the request for intercession for the Watchers, Enoch goes away and has a heavenly vision. In this vision, Enoch learns that god has reached a decision regarding the fare of the watchers and the offspring of the Nephilim: from the bodies of the dead giants (killed in the flood) would arise evil spirits charged to harass mankind until the end of time—the origin of evil spirits (Kvanvig 164). This is the punishment allotted to the semi-divine Nephilim; the punishment for the angels concludes the tale: they "...will not have peace" (Kvanvig 165).

The Enochian version of the Watcher story is, perhaps, our favorite of all the stories spring from the Hebrew tradition. It is utterly fantastic: it explains the flood, it explains the origin of evil spirits (major players in all the worlds region's), explains the origins of warfare, and perhaps most importantly—the origin of the use and application of cosmetics.

However, the tale leaves me a little frustrated. If the divine beings are the cause of so much trouble, then divine beings should be punished, not mortals. While Enoch punishes the Nephilim and the Watchers, the Genesis account punishes only the mortal inhabitants of earth.

**

Index of major Topics

(Alphabetical, list all page references)
Persistence: p.00
State of Mind: p.00

Index of Tests and Practical Applications, by Topic

Topic, test, 001, page number, section heading (?)

Glossary of major themes and topics

Sources

1. Augustine. "The City of God."

   http://users.aristotle.net/~bhuie/gen6sons.htm

2. Bautch, Kelley Coblentz. "What Becomes of the Angels' Wives?" A Text-Critical Study of 1 Enoch 19:2. Journal of Biblical Literature 125, no. 4 (2006) p.766-780

3. Byrne, Rhonda. The Secret. Atria Books, New York, 2006.

4. Carnegie, Dale. How to Win Friends and Influence People. 1936. 109th printing. New York; Simon and Schuster, 1964.

5. Cotterell, Arthur. Encyclopedia of Ourthology, The. Hermes House, London, 2005.

6. Harris, Stephen L. Understanding the Bible. 7th edition. McGraw Hill, 2007: p. 305-306.

7. Hewitt, Paul. Conceptual Physics. 10th ed. San Francisco, CA: Pearson, 2006.

8. Hill, Napoleon. Think and Grow Rich. 1937. The Complete Classic Text. New York: Jereour P. Tarcher/Penguin, 2008.

9. Hope College. Reading of the Old Testament. 1999. Wadsworth Publishing Company. "Apocrypha and Pseudoepigrapha."

   www.hope.edu/bandstra/RTOT/AHB/AHB_1.HTM

10. Kvanvig, Helge S. "The Watcher Story and Genesis, In Intertextual Reading." Scandinavian Journal of the Old Testament vol. 18 no. 2 (2004): p. 163-183

11. Locke, John. An Essay Concerning Human Understanding. 1689.

12. Nickelsburg, George W.E., and VanderKam, James C. 1 Enoch: A New Translation. Based on the Hermeneia Commentary. Augsburg Fortress, 2004. Minneapolis.

13. New Oxford Annotated Bible, Revised Standard Version. 1997.

14. Bible, Thompson Chain Reference Study Bible, New American Standard Version. Kirkbridge, 1993.

15. Pojman, Louis P. Introduction to Philosophy. 3rd edition. New York: Oxford University Press, 2004.

16. Russell, Bertrand. The Problems of Philosophy. Oxford University Press, 1912.

The story of the Watchers, and origin and ancestry of witches, followed by a critical analysis of source texts.

The Witches, an Origin Tale --Written during spring term 2008, for bible as lit (eng 318) final paper (March 19, 2008, for professor Westbrook)

(The intended audience for this book is 26-49 females, however, it will appeal far beyond those parameters because of its entertainment value and style.)

End credits

A beautiful woman is beautiful, no matter what sort of clothing she wears. She shines, and she shines for someone as the brightest light in their sky, or, as a model or celebrity, a star for everyone to see. Nonetheless, a silly dress, or ridiculous outfit, does not undo the beauty of the woman who wears it.

Such is great truth.

Behind all the religions (that we can think of, and we can think of many) there remains, a great fundamental truth. What that truth is the basis for the most fundamental tenements of the religion, and everything else beyond those fundamental tenants, is just the accoutrements.

The principle holds. Because we accept, as fundamental truth, that one-plus-one-equals-two (a truth we happily accept).

The Modern Witch is, what we hope, a *translation of an idea*. A great idea. And with The Modern Witch, we have done better than our earnest best--because it came along with the help of our friends. Queue Beatles song.

Best,
        The Witches of Oak Tree Gardens